THE YEAR
OF THE
REVOLUTIONARY
NEW BREAD-MAKING
MACHINE

Hassan Daoud

The Year
of the
Revolutionary
New Bread-Making
Machine

Translated from the Arabic by
Randa Jarrar

TELEGRAM
London San Francisco Beirut

First published in Arabic in 1996 as *Sanat al-Automatic*
by Dar an-Nahar, Beirut

This edition published 2007 by Telegram Books

ISBN: 978-1-84659-026-9

A full CIP record for this book is available from the British Library.
A full CIP record for this book is available from the Library of Congress.

Manufactured in Lebanon

TELEGRAM
26 Westbourne Grove, London W2 5RH
825 Page Street, Suite 203, Berkeley, California 94710
Tabet Building, Mneimneh Street, Hamra, Beirut
www.telegrambooks.com

For Rashid Zabeeb

'They were stricken with a rainless year; a year of drought.'
From *Lisan al-'Arab* ('The Arab Tongue')

1

At the building's third floor I told Ramez it was here that I'd seen him in a dream. He was standing on the third or fourth step of the stairs, surrounded by Kurdish women in traditional dress, with their keffiyeh-like headscarves. Ramez had fallen into their grasp after I'd narrowly escaped it, and I now stood watching him from the stairs above. They reached out to him, as though to pull at his flesh. He was glued to the banister in fear, but somehow managed to peel himself from it, stick out his chest, and flex the muscles in his arms, just like the body-builder in the tattoo he'd gotten a few days before on his left arm. Then he flipped in mid-air, like a wrestler, and kept doing so, back and forth, until the Kurdish women disappeared without a trace.

Farhat wanted him to show us the tattoo again. The swelling from the needle had gone down and the muscle man was beginning to settle into his final shape. The lower half was thin because the tattooist had only really focused on the chest and arms. It didn't resemble Ramez's body at all, which was slim and tall.

'Don't bring the tattoo to the gym or it'll show you up!' Farhat told Ramez.

I laughed, but Khalil, who, according to my father, is a relative of ours, didn't. He had a smile on his face the whole way back from the bakery and would widen it a bit, in curiosity or confusion, whenever any of us spoke to him.

Except for a single apartment on the bottom floor, the building was empty. Its residents had gone to the mountains for the summer holidays. But still we didn't dare ring the doorbells to entertain ourselves with the sounds of their songs playing within. On the fourth floor, Farhat asked, 'Is this where Aida lives?' Aida of the white legs. When I told him that it was, he stuck his face against the doorknob where her hand often rested. Ramez bet that when Farhat lifted his head from the doorknob Khalil would stare through the keyhole and try to see what was inside. The moment we glimpsed the door to my apartment on the fifth floor, we raced to it, running to see who'd get there first.

Our apartment was empty like the others, and dirty as well since my parents had left. Farhat opened the door to the fridge, even though he knew it was empty. Then he asked me, as he did every day, if the tap water was good enough to drink. He brought his lips to the tap to take a drink, and as he did so the dizziness in my head grew and buzzed loudly, like a large fly.

'You'll be like that until your blood gets used to the tobacco,' Ramez said, and gave me a cigarette from the pack he hid in his sock. 'Smoke,' he said, as though I could get used to it quicker than the usual two weeks, at the end of which, according to him, I'd stop getting dizzy. He blew two thick columns of smoke from his nostrils to demonstrate that he'd beaten me in spades at this particular game.

We'd left the record player on in the sitting room, and Umm Kulthum's voice rose suddenly from the speakers. *Baghdad, the lions' lair, the lair of eternal majesty ... esty ... esty ... esty.*

'It's scratched,' I shouted to Farhat from the hallway, and asked him to turn off the record player, which looked like a handbag. But Farhat just lifted the needle and placed it at the record's midpoint to start it all over again. It scratched again loudly and we almost came to blows when I ripped the record player's cord from the socket.

'He asked you to turn the record player *off*,' Ramez told Farhat as he approached him from behind me.

Khalil was going from room to room, admiring their size and stopping at the Western-style bathroom where he did nothing in particular but stare at its contents. Ramez had followed him in there the night before and seen him spitting from the small balcony, then leaning his head forward to see if he could spot the gob landing on the street below. He was so absorbed in this that he'd almost fallen over the rails. When Farhat and I went to check on him, he had grown bored of the game and of the balcony.

We all congregated in the living room. Khalil didn't stop for us but kept on walking.

After that, we took the record player out onto the big balcony, which overlooked all the buildings, and Ramez warned Farhat not to play the Baghdad record since it might damage the needle. Then he told him that I was well able to turn the record player on myself.

Khalil watched me as I lowered the needle. Before the music started, Farhat asked Ramez for a cigarette. He gave us all one, except Khalil, who doesn't smoke. *I am the people, I am the people and I know not the impossible.* Farhat asked me to turn up the volume, even though we were all hunched around the record player. 'I know not the impossible,' Ramez sang along with Umm Kulthum. Farhat asked me to turn it up again, moving his wrists up and down with the song's melody ... *My country, my country, is open like the sky*. As I sang, I looked around me at the buildings that separated us from the large, empty dump, to measure its distance and see whether the music would reach it. Nothing changed in the buildings around us, none of the darkened rooms lit up.

Ramez turned his hand to Khalil to urge him to sing, and Khalil hummed as he stood and sang a word or two from the song. 'I am the people, I am the people.'

Ramez sang more than the rest of us. Then he turned it down, right in the middle of the song's emotional crescendo, and announced to us that he was going to steal the bakery's delivery van one night. He turned the volume back up and joined in the singing once more: 'I am the people, I am the people and I know not ...'

The sounds filled the cavernous space between the buildings, lit by a few apartment windows opposite. Ramez brought out a box of cigarettes and threw some at us. We put them in our mouths, but left them unlit.

When the first side of the album was over, Farhat announced that we should stay up all night. But they didn't let kids into casinos, Ramez said, grasping my hand before I could flip the record over. They both asked me to start it from the beginning. *I am the people, I am the people* ... It was as though Umm Kulthum, as she began the same song all over again, had grown tired and weary of singing it. Ramez, however, kept up his singing with the same intensity. And we all knew he'd keep going till the end of the record if he could, trying to win a bet that no one had challenged him to. He carried on on his own, ending each word with fervent emphasis, just to show us that he was still into it. But then he turned down the volume to say something to Farhat and it was obvious he was bored of singing too and that he'd lost the imaginary bet.

He told Farhat that if he wanted to, he could stay up at the bakery.

'Take a cab there and tell the driver to wait for you at the door,' he joked.

Khalil, who towered above us, laughed at this, a sudden outburst which he muffled quickly.

'You're laughing at me, you idiot?' Farhat asked.

Khalil didn't answer, but turned and went to the sitting room.

Ramez looked Farhat in the eye and asked him why he'd called Khalil an idiot. 'That idiot could break your bones if he wanted to,' and they almost started fighting.

He was the real idiot, Farhat answered, because only an idiot would tattoo a dwarf on his arm. I stayed well out of it, turning off the record player, folding it up and carrying it away, so that they'd think I didn't care if they fought, and that I was just leaving to clear the way for them. Khalil was standing alone behind the sitting room door, thinking about what Farhat had said to him. I said nothing, but reached out to Farhat on the balcony and pulled him into the apartment, asking him to come and talk to Khalil.

Ramez and I took Khalil to the sitting room and let him stretch out and sleep on the couch, hiding his face with a cushion so he wouldn't worry about us seeing him through the open door. We turned the lights off on the balcony, so we could undress, and then made up the cots, unfolding them and lifting down the blankets and pillows. We were all stretched out, our heads stuck between the rails of the balcony. Ramez said he was out of cigarettes and was going to keep the last one for himself. I kept my eyes wide open and my head to one side to keep the dizziness and its loud buzz at bay, but it only got worse as soon as I got under the covers. Ramez, scolding Farhat and making up with him, told him that Khalil understood things and that he should leave him alone. Then he gave him a drag from his cigarette, and he tried to pass it along to me but I pushed his hand away because the dizziness had expanded in my head.

Before we fell asleep, a light went on in a window of the building across the way, its soft glow from that distance brushing our white blankets and revealing their brightness over us. Farhat flipped over and faced the light, and before his eyes even landed on the window, he said, 'It's the blonde.' Ramez and I turned over as well. It was her, and she stood right in the middle of the frame, close to the window. She stood for a while with her back to us, as if she was talking to someone in the room, but then she turned and looked out of the window for a long time, as though the other person had left through a door out of view. She leaned forward and lowered her hands, as though she were taking her clothes off, and Ramez said she would do what she did the night before. Farhat said we should wake Khalil, as if sharing this with him would erase their argument, but Ramez told him to let him sleep.

She turned around and faced the same spot inside the room again, and her naked lower half was out of view again. Farhat asked me if the door to the roof was unlocked, and he craned his neck to see through the rails, but knew that it wouldn't be the right angle to see her, so he gave up. Still facing the same spot inside the room, it seemed as though she were the one talking this time, but without moving her arms or thrusting her head forwards. Ramez said she was all alone and that she was putting on a show for us. She reached her arms back and took her top off, and Farhat asked me, just like he did the night before, if there was a pair of binoculars in the apartment. Suddenly, she left the room and followed an inaudible voice coming from within the apartment. We stared at the empty window, and Ramez said that she hadn't turned the light off. Then he shivered, and was embarrassed by his arousal, and to cover it up he said that she was just giving us a small intermission like the one they have at the movies.

She never came back. But we sat on the balcony and waited, our heads between the railings, trying to get a glimpse of the two breasts we'd seen the night before. They were large, and she'd stood in the same place, busily turning something over in her hands, her breasts rising and falling in a gentle movement. Farhat mimicked their movement with his hands, raising them and dropping them in front of his chest. We fell asleep intermittently, and in our dreams saw her breasts in the brightly lit room, and so we kept waking up and looking across to the window, only to find the light on in the room but the window empty. I don't know which of us gave up first, or when all three of us had sunken into a deep sleep, but soon enough, not a single one of us remained awake.

2

When my father took me down to the bakery, my mother said it would ruin me the way it ruined my brother. He was one school year ahead of me, despite the fact that he was two whole years older. On the day he came home with his final report card (after which he never went back to school) my father read out the marks, one by one, in his loudest voice, and asked him, after each one, what exactly he'd been doing in class when the assignment was being given, or why he hadn't passed, or why his friends had passed and he'd failed. My brother stood in front of him in grown-up clothes; 'cloaked in shattered hopes,' as my father would say. He always resembled someone on his way to a bakery, not just during recesses and weekends, but in school hours as well.

He stood silently, not knowing what to say. My father, who always spoke his mind – which in effect caused all his children to talk like grown-ups – told my relatives that my older brother had declared that he didn't want to go back to school, and that he would be lying if he said he did. Ramez had dropped out too, and so had Mustafa, whose father's bakery wasn't very far from ours. My very tall uncle used to say, from his post high above the heads of our relatives, that the boys left schools for bakeries because they liked to eat hot, fresh bread. He was talking about something I didn't yet have the capacity to understand.

Whenever my mother claimed that the bakery would ruin me, my father asked her how stacking bread, two-by-two on a wooden board, could be the undoing of anyone. In the bakery, I stood at the end of the oven, far away from the workers, loaves of swollen bread arriving from the baker who would toss them at me. I just stacked them as though I were counting. Whenever the board got full, I'd ask the worker, using his language, to pick the board up. This, in my Mother's opinion, would ruin me, because speaking with the counter boys was just like saying curse words. According to her, I should just pick up the board, which towers with bread, and slam it down against the one beneath it, so that the delivery guy, hearing the noise, would come over to get it.

It was not just the two-by-two stacking of the loaves, but the talk with the counter boys, and their ways, and how I stood within earshot of the baker, who cursed every time the worker took too long to hand him the balls of dough – the baker, who propelled large wads of spit from his mouth, not caring that I stood close to him as he did. All these things would ruin me, as would the bathroom of the bakery, which stood on the floor above the oven, its dirt and smells, and the insects that came out from its cracks every time I opened the door.

My brother may have learned our mother's ways of knowing what ruins a person, because he didn't like people who spoke drunkenly, or had black and rotten teeth. Once, he told me to stay away from a worker whose breath stank, because he thought the boy had become that way by destroying his body with filthy habits. My brother began to stand in my father's place, selling bread to customers, and talking to the counter boys from the small window at his side. That's where he would peer at me from, as I stacked bread whenever they took me with them to the bakery. When he wrote, in his typical handwriting, 'In the name of God, most Merciful' on the face of the big accounting book whose pages turned every day, my brother became an authority and a stand-in for my father and uncle at the bakery.

His time of ruin was short. Or maybe he was only ruined once, and came out of it without learning how to smoke or talk about girls as if he really had something to say. 'My son isn't ruined,' my father answered each time my mother said that my going to the bakery would ruin me as it had ruined my brother. Then he would ask her if my brother was anything like Ramez, who had left school and didn't even want to work at the bakery. That was all he could say against Ramez, because it was all he really knew about him, which he concluded simply from his appearance. He didn't like the way Ramez laughed – he called it a hash-addict's laugh – or the way he kept his wages from the bakery in his pocket, as though he were just another worker in his brother's bakery. On the way to work, my father always asked me who cooked for Ramez, washed his clothes, and told him not to stay out too late at night. I'd answer that he ate at his sister's house, that he sent his dirty clothes to be washed at his brothers' houses, and that I didn't know whether he stayed up late. Then my father would say that he didn't understand how a boy of that age could live without his parents.

He didn't like me to go out with Ramez, or even talk to him. Just like he didn't want me to go out with Farhat, who he thought was a bad kid, even though he'd never actually seen him do anything wrong. In the car, on our way to the bakery, I'd wonder if he was right about Farhat, or if he knew something about Ramez that he didn't say in front of me.

It was a relief to know that I was not like them, that I was a good kid who really didn't do anything wrong. And I truly believed that I *was* good, not just in his eyes, but in those of our relatives as well.

I stand and stare at the floor when my aunt's husband teases me and tenderly slaps the back of my neck, and I also act shyly at Farhat's house, and follow him from room to room while he looks for his clothes. The last time I was there, his mother didn't see me coming in behind him, and she said that she didn't want him to hang out with 'that bad kid,' and she would have said a whole lot more if I hadn't appeared behind Farhat at the kitchen door. Instead, she bent

over me. 'Oh! Hello, sweetheart,' she said. 'How are your parents?
Do send them my love!'

3

My father wanted all his workers to be like Mr Logs, whom he brought by our house before taking to the bakery. First of all, he admired his name, even though the ovens were no longer fuelled by logs and now ran on gas instead. In any case, this didn't lessen his admiration for the name, which belonged to the man who dwarfed all others in his strength. The man didn't deny his name when he came over to the house. He was tall, as tall as my father. And his handshake was strong and coarse from working with the oven's hot winds and its heavy metal tongs. On top of all that, he was in my father's favourite age range, the one my own father belonged to, where men don't find anything funny unless it happened to the ancients. And, just like ancient men, these two began to give each other compliments as they started to eat, and they shared the full water jug as though they were exchanging precious gifts every single time it passed hands.

Mr Logs left our house wearing the blue suit that had hung in my father's wardrobe with the rest of the clothes. It looked good on him, and he kept checking the way it covered his body, and how some of the buttons were fastened and others were not. He would turn to the left and then the right to see what the suit looked like from different angles, front and back. My father told him to go and look at himself in the mirror in the bedroom, but he murmured something that suggested he was too shy to do so. The blue suit looked better on him than it ever did on my father. It was like the suit had never been worn before. And when he left the house in it and went down the stairs, my father kept repeating, 'Allah!' in low and high tones, as if he were listening to a recitation of the *Qu'ran*.

He was the age my father liked men to be. And he was in the shape men his age are supposed to be in. At one point, my father wanted to give Zeid the worker – who is the same age as Mr Logs – some clothes. So he sent my brother to our house, rather than go himself. My brother asked me, sending his voice up the empty stairwell between the five floors, to throw down some clothes for Zeid since his had rotted on his body. I asked, sending my voice down in return, if he meant I should give him my own clothes. He became furious and began to shout so loud that I'd understood that I should send him anything, any clothes at all.

I thought Zeid's face was a beautiful one, with his soft hair and his straight nose; he looked like an American employee passing by the bakery on his way to the university. Watching him among the workers, I decided that he was different from them, not just because of the way he looked, but because of the knowledge I'm sure he had but didn't share, since he was quiet most of the time. As he worked, moving between the scaffolds and the oven, he looked young, and lifting the boards up in his arms his movements resembled those of a lean dancer. But my father must not have noticed any of this, because he only talked to him about work, and when he paid him, at the end of each day, he didn't joke with him the way he did with the other workers.

At the bakery the next afternoon, my brother never explained to me how Zeid's clothes could rot on his very flesh. He just said, in a way that showed that he found my confusion strange, that they rotted, as simple as that, as if everyone in the world knew how clothes rotted on bodies.

When he described Zeid to me, my father used a slang word that people his age never normally did; he said, 'Zeid is *touched*,' pursing his lips and knotting his brow so that the word would mean 'sick'. I decided, once again, that there were certain people I understood that my father never would. But then I saw Zeid transferring boards between the scaffolds wearing my clothes, which were short and tight on him. He didn't leave the shirt unbuttoned, so that he could move more freely, but had it all done up, disregarding the fact that the tightness of the clothes on his thin body made his head look much too big for his skinny body.

Zeid seemed handsome for two months, then it was over. He would stand in the front room with the customers in complete silence, one hand over the other, and wouldn't come back into the work area until my father asked him, angrily, what he was doing out there. Two months, then he changed. It was as though he hadn't worked at the bakery at all. In this way, I began to believe that what I saw in him was just a figment of my imagination; like I had mixed together all the images I had memorised, and had placed Zeid in the shoes of another man entirely.

4

Ramez showed up in the Fiat, weaving at the intersection and almost crashing into the kerb. He was holding the steering wheel with both hands, with his head lowered, the way car-jackers do. He looked back and gave us a look that said *hurry up*, then focused straight ahead once we started running towards him; it was as if he was just as afraid as on the day he'd stolen the car from in front of the bakery. He lost patience when he saw us fighting over the front seat, and honked loudly on the horn to get us away from the door. Then he turned the steering wheel angrily, but we refused to let go of the door, until he said he'd leave without us, putting his foot down noisily on the gas.

I got in first, followed by Muhammad who sat next to me, then Farhat, stubbornly, who didn't like being left out, nor the fact that he was sitting alone in the back seat with Khalil.

Ramez only needed a few metres to accelerate to full speed. He told Muhammad not to lean into him, then lifted his hand up to the horn, lowering his head as though he were being chased by police. He didn't say a word until we were far away from the neighbourhoods where his brother hung out. Muhammad spoke though, after we'd crossed two or three streets, and teasingly told Farhat to relax since he was sitting in the backseat. Ramez said nothing, and Farhat leaned against the door, its window rolled to the top. Before we reached the gas station, Muhammad told Khalil to get closer to Farhat, that there was too great a distance between them. Khalil smiled at him, but Ramez gave Muhammad a look that said he'd do something to him if he didn't stop kidding around.

'Two liras,' Muhammad said when Ramez parked in front of the pump, and each of us gave him the money for gas. Khalil tried to pay, but Ramez looked at him in the rearview mirror and said, 'No, Khalil,' then got out of the car and stood next to the gas station attendant as he pumped fuel into the car, put water into the radiator, and checked the tyres for air. Ramez rubbed his hands together as he got back into the car, but before he took off he pushed Muhammad towards me, and told him to stick by me and get away from him. He wasn't in a hurry this time; we were at the edge of Beirut and his brother would never find us here.

When we got to the first wide road that led to the mountains, Ramez was going as fast as he could. The car was elevated at the back like a small bus, so that it had plenty of room for all the bread he distributed to restaurants and groceries. But Ramez was now using it to race cars out of his way, passing tightly between them and the sides of the road. Whenever we'd pass by a car so close we almost touched it, we'd wave to whoever was driving it and they'd let us pass. Muhammad would clap his hands and break into song, in a voice that always made it sound like he was making fun of whatever he was singing.

He told Ramez to sing, when we were on the wide, flat road with the mountains surrounding us. Ramez took a long, hard drag on his cigarette and released the heavy smoke from his nostrils. Instead of singing, he told us all not to leave any cigarette butts in the car's ashtrays for his brother to find. 'How can you blame me?' Muhammad sang, encouraging Ramez, but again he sounded like he was making fun of the song. 'Just clap,' Ramez told him, as he prepared himself to imitate Abdel Halim's voice. *How can you blame me? Mmm, how can you blame me? If you saw her eyes, Mmm, if you saw her eyes, Mmm.* Muhammad began humming the melody and

singing along with the *Mmm*s, while clapping his hands and raising
them so that we would too. But we neither clapped nor sang, so
he raised his voice, going out of tune completely. Farhat raised his
voice behind us, and sang along in a way that ruined the song but let
us know that he was no longer miffed about sitting in the back seat.
Ramez gave him a look that told him to get in tune. Muhammad
leaned his arm against me, then against Ramez, as though he were
doing a seated dance. Ramez shook his head and rolled his eyes at
Khalil in the rearview mirror, who smiled broadly and was on the
verge of clapping along with us.

The Fiat was letting cars pass by now, and our voices, when we
all joined in, were loud. The people in the cars stared at us. Khalil
sang quietly, in case we all stopped singing and left him to sing
alone. At the end of each song Ramez would tell us that his voice
used to be much better and that it'd been ruined by all the smoking.
Muhammad asked him why he didn't have a radio in the car. Ramez
promised that the next time he saw his brother he'd tell him to
install a radio so he wouldn't have to hear Muhammad sing.

By the time we reached Aley the Fiat was going as fast as it could;
Ramez hadn't hit the brakes at all from the top of the hill. It was like
a box being pulled along by the small engine under its narrow, short
hood. We stopped singing when we reached the roundabout where
we always got confused, and asked Ramez if we should keep going
straight through Aley or up the road to the higher mountains. We
already knew Aley, Farhat said, and there was nothing to do there.
On previous visits we'd driven down the strip where all the shops
and restaurants and bars were, but never actually stopped the car
and got out. Muhammad said we should go down the strip again
and drive under the trees planted along the middle. Ramez asked
me what I thought, and I suggested that we drive down to the end of
the trees and back, to the wide roundabout. In the past, we had no
idea where to park the car, not only because of traffic, but because
we didn't know where to go. We were not like the locals, who lived
in amongst the shops and restaurants.

'Let's go down to the trees,' Muhammad told Ramez.

Ramez drove quickly up and down the strip so that we could look at it from both directions: going down, and going back up again. Aley was exactly as we'd last seen it. The leaves of its trees were light, their colours changed from the wind that shook their branches, like an arm jingling and jangling bracelets and anklets.

We passed by the hotel, whose roof was the only visible part from the strip, and Ramez asked, 'Do you know how much it costs per night to stay there?'

'Probably around sixty liras,' we said, a made-up figure that we seemed to have all agreed upon the last time we visited.

Then he asked us if breakfast was included in that price and if not, how much it was, for those of us who only wanted to have breakfast there. Muhammad said that the price depended on how many eggs you had. Ramez was preparing to tell us a joke, but we hadn't answered him in a way that encouraged joke-telling.

'How much for a single boiled egg?' he asked, directing the question solely at Muhammad.

'Three liras, but it's four if you want salt with it,' came the reply.

Ramez said, 'I'll eat three eggs and tell them to go to the bakery and get my week's wages from my brother.'

Muhammad laughed as though he were mocking laughter itself, then he told Ramez once again to buy a car radio, and pointed to where it should go. In the back seat the wind was blowing so hard through the window it lifted Khalil's hair off his forehead, which was too big for him. His eyes were half-open and he looked like he was shunning the wind and welcoming it all at once. Ramez saw him in the rearview and asked him if he was sleepy, and Muhammad turned to face Khalil, asking, in that voice of his, if he ever got car sick. Khalil smiled and shook his head to get Muhammad off his back. Then he looked at Farhat, who was leaning his head against the glass of the partially opened window, as though waiting for Farhat to ask him something. Once Khalil was sure we were going to leave him alone, he went back to his previous position, fighting and surrendering to the wind.

We couldn't find the small side street we'd stopped at the last time, the day we'd stolen cherries from the trees planted to its right. After hesitating in front of several side streets, Farhat said that we wouldn't find it unless we headed back.

'But we're not going back the same way,' Muhammad said, and suggested that we find a new road home.

Ramez agreed and stepped on the gas, then asked Muhammad to light him a cigarette.

If it weren't for all the cars that crowded the streets, we would've driven past the restaurants and cafés at the same high speed. And we knew nothing of the summer cabins except for the streets on which we drove past, towards even more cabins. In the new town, just like in Aley, we had no idea where to stop. I remained silent when Ramez eyed the doorways and patios of cafés because I was embarrassed to get out of the car – meant for work and not play – in front of the tourists. Ramez reamed off the names of villages as we drove through them, just to show off that he'd driven through them before. When he said that we'd reach Armoun before Beirut, the empty road ahead seemed less lonely. We knew we'd get out in Armoun, parking the car in the heavily wooded streets, in which the trees resembled identical hiding places. Farhat said he hoped we'd run into the three girls that we'd seen last time, who'd gone for a walk away from their parents. Khalil hadn't been with us that day. After parking the car under the pine trees, we'd seen them strolling and chatting. Muhammad said that he would talk to them, but he didn't have the guts to, not until he followed them alone and had Farhat walk a few steps behind him. Returning, they told us that Muhammad had talked to the girls, who laughed and weaved from side to side in single file.

'What was her name again?' Muhammad asked, 'the slim red head?'

'Her name was Susan,' Farhat replied.

But Ramez accused them of making the whole thing up; they'd surely invented the name. Afterwards, he headed back to the car, shaking the keys in his hand like a matador.

5

My father installed a window in the wall to his right, so he no longer had to leave his spot in the front to talk to the bakery's workers. The window was tiny and fitted only his head, which he thrust in whenever he wanted to say something to them. They'd both turn to look at him at the same time, away from the high stone table, which stayed clean because of the dough's moisture. These were the strongest workers in the bakery, and when he referred to them as the stone-table duo, I knew he was intentionally leaving off the third worker; not because he would switch from the table to the scaffold to the oven, but because his body, skinny from constant movement, wasn't built as well as theirs. The table workers were even stronger than the bakers, who would fight over the oven and leave it after a week, or a couple of months or so. The bakers pulled back and forth, pushing the dough and pulling at their metal tongs, leaning right into the oven. They spent their entire day at this. This made them skinny. Their strength wasn't in their muscles, but right in their bones, which Abu Deeb kept firm and straight whenever he walked between the oven and my father's spot in the front. And it was in their height, and in the way they never got ill. Abu Saeed was especially good at that; in order to bear the heat which blazed in front of his face and chest, he cooled his back off with a fan which he'd placed behind him on a shelf.

When Abu Saeed worked, he was hot in front and cold in the back. My father, who thought no one should be this way, told him that he would get sick. But Abu Saeed, who said he knew his body well, didn't ever catch a cold or get sick, and he wouldn't listen to anyone who suggested his eyesight was weak because of the differences in the temperature of his body. He'd stand and watch my father from behind those thick lenses that made his eyes look large and wide, and he never brought his head in close to look at something, the way other people who wear thick glasses do.

'You're killing yourself,' my father would say to him. Abu Saeed wouldn't respond, but would wave his hand in a way that said, 'Nothing remains, and what doesn't perish from the wind will surely perish otherwise.' Then, my father would give him a cigarette from the pack, which Abu Saeed would bring right up to his nostrils before lighting. He wouldn't leave the front of the bakery unless there were too many female customers and my father kept glancing at his bare chest and back, and his long, thin legs.

The bakers' strength didn't lie in their muscles, but in the way their bodies differed from the bodies of other men we knew. But my father noticed that their strength only lasted a month or two, and then they left, and it was the same with the bread delivery men. After midnight, if any of them were over an hour late my father knew that they would never show up, and he'd drive to the bakers' neighbourhood and hire a new one, or he'd go to the bakers' café, even though the kinds of men who frequented it only worked about two or three days, and then he'd have to go back to the bakers' neighbourhood again. My father would leave his car and walk to their rooms, which were like tents, and he'd call to them by name. They'd come out and tell him they needed to sleep since they hadn't gotten any rest during the day, or that another bakery owner was due to pick them up later, or that their small sick child just fell asleep half an hour earlier.

He worried also that if they left work at noon they wouldn't return that night. As he'd say, he only had the table trio. They stood side by side, the dough-maker, dough-cutter, and dough-roller, their backs to the wall that separated the stone table from the front room.

The first things my father saw as he slid the small window open were their strong backs. Even when they'd turn to talk to him, he could still see their strong backs hulking behind them. They were the stoutest workers there. Even the dough-cutter, who stood in the middle, was sturdy and muscular despite his short build. My father made him taller by placing a rock, which resembled a piece of cut marble, under his feet. Yet he wasn't a dwarf; his arms were of normal length and his legs weren't bowed, and when he spoke he was no different from men with bodies of average height.

'His body is small,' my father would say, drawing with his hands the shape of a ball, signifying his slightness and attitude in that one motion. The strongest parts of his body were the edges of his palms with which he cut the dough into balls and weighed out the loaves. Once my brother and I said that they were like rocks, and he laughed. Then he stared at them and said they were made of dead flesh. The three of them never left the stone table, unless Nawwaf the dough-maker wanted to stretch his legs after moving the 100-kilo bags of flour and emptying them into the wide-lipped machine, or if Ghaleb the dough-cutter went to the bathroom after filling the table with unbaked loaves, or Hussein the shorty rubbed his palms together to remove the moist pieces of dough from between his fingers.

They took a few short steps slowly, hardly exerting their muscles at all, so they could get some rest from work, which my brother had begun seeing as exercise since he started going to the gym. To him there was no difference between the bakery and the gym. He said their bodies were stronger than athletes,' because they exercised them twelve hours a day. My brother would break down their body parts according to their movements, saying, for example, that Ghaleb's forearms were stronger than Nawwaf's, who had the better back and shoulders. Before he went to the gym, he had begun to do things the way they did: he'd exercise at work, turning to the paper bags without moving his legs off the floor, since, according to him, this strengthened the waist and stomach, the way turning the entire head to the back strengthened all the muscles in your neck.

6

The delivery men were quick at work and quick to escape the bakery. For that reason, my father wanted to make sure that there was room for at least one of them to spend the night, and he let him sleep on top of the flour bags. The dough-cutter would wake him up as soon as the yeast rose, and the delivery man would jump up immediately as though the dough-cutter had saved him from falling into a coma. But after he'd given the cutter a good, long look, he'd go back to sleep on top of the bags.

'Five minutes,' my father would tell the cutter, who'd climbed up to the sleeping area to bring him down. The delivery man would talk to the cutter in his sleep, to prolong his nap-time. Sometimes my father woke him up by yelling up to him, in a loud voice that vibrated against the wide ceiling and shook as it quieted down, like the shaking of a large watermelon. He didn't shut up when he heard the delivery man's voice answer him from above, because he knew he'd just go back to sleep.

'Adeeb,' he'd yell (if the delivery man was Adeeb). 'Adeeb, Adeeb, Adeeb. You've gone back to sleep, Adeeb.'

He'd tell him to be careful when walking among the flour bags, and asked him to wash his face in the bathroom. Then he'd say, 'Are you washing your face, Adeeb?' And Adeeb would answer in a voice just loud enough for my father to hear, that he would, and that way he helped himself stay awake.

My father liked it when they slept at the bakery, because he hated having to go down to al-Wata, or the bakers' café which was filled with gamblers and card players, and he hated waiting for Zeid who refused to tell him where he slept, except to say that it was by the sea shore. Knowing they were asleep at the bakery, he slept in peace, without the anxiety and worry that made him talk in his sleep, and raise his head off the pillow and shout, 'Is the delivery man here?'

If they spent the night at the bakery, my father got to work on time.

'Just like any other worker,' he told my mother, who complained in turn, 'But who else goes to work at one in the morning?'

Then she'd start her broken record, and tell him to find someone else to work the night shift instead of him, and he'd look at her with his puffy eyes, and tie his belt quickly around his pants, hurrying to leave.

The workers who slept at the bakery lived there as well, exactly the way kids live in houses and don't leave them except to go to the store and back. And like kids in houses, they got bored at the bakery, and spent their free time going from the front to the back, between the stove and the oven. They looked like they were waiting for the outing they'd never go on, all dressed up in their clothes that didn't look like work clothes. Besides, going out would ruin them, as my father liked to say when he came to the bakery and found them gone. He'd picture them at the bakers' café, or at the market where women would get them sick.

My father would visit the oven late in the afternoon to check that the yeast seller had come by with the yeast; to make sure that there was enough bread; to see what the workers were doing. Just as he'd worry that they'd go bad if they left the bakery, he felt we'd go bad if we stayed in it with them. He judged them by their looks, and told us not to go near Zeid, whom my father forced to stay in the bakery, or he'd ask Adeeb not to go out in the front, where my brother and

I stood, so that he wouldn't use 'grown-up' language with us. When it came to Muhammad El-Halaby, he distrusted both his looks and his voice.

Muhammad was twenty-five but he sang like a fifteen-year-old while he worked or took a break. He used to say he wanted to be a singer, and this in front of my father, who thought that this meant he frequented clubs like the Fontana by the Ain El-Murayisa shore.

After spending half an hour singing all the tunes he knew, he'd fall silent, then look at me and say, 'Your turn. Why don't you sing?' Realising that I didn't know any songs, he'd tell me to just sing along with him, and he'd sing slowly as though spelling the words out to me. I joined him in saying the words, but I was too embarrassed to sing them the way he did with his nice voice. He enjoyed it, or at least he said he did so as not to make me feel bad. Then he asked me to join him on back-up, and harmonised, making faces to signify the harmonies, thinking this would help me. But when that failed too, he simply said we should try again another time.

He believed that if I just memorised the words to his songs, my voice would become beautiful.

'That's what it's like in Halab, my hometown,' he said. But even when I memorised the verses my voice stayed the same.

'Something is trapping your voice,' he said, then released a long tone to show me that nothing had trapped his.

One time he said that my voice was suitable for modern love songs, and it was as though he'd hatefully knocked me down a notch to that lower rung of music. I had a sentimental voice like Abdel Halim Hafez or Muharram Fouad, he said. On this lesser, sentimental perch a singer needs to add nothing to his pretty voice but mawkishness. It was true that when I sang Abdel Halim songs I sounded much better. Still, Muhammad decided that during those afternoons, when we worked together in the front of the bakery, he would sing alone. He was sure that I'd knock him out of tune, since it was his opinion that those with inferior voices didn't like to hear others sing.

He did, however, succeed in teaching me the art of smoking. I used to pull on his cigarette and exhale through my mouth.

'Not like that,' he'd say, then, taking a long draw, he'd bring his face close to mine so I could see how he inhaled, then exhaled, mouth open, a tall, thick cloud. After I learned how to do this myself, it was my duty to relax while smoking, and to sit back the way those who enjoy smoking do. I hadn't yet had an entire cigarette when I went to visit Ramez at his brother's bakery, to brag that I'd learned how to smoke. He wanted to make sure I wasn't lying, so he lit one and gave it to me. I took an extended drag and let the smoke out of my mouth and nostrils. Then I took another, even longer one, at the end of which the back of my throat burned, and I began huffing since I was still out of breath from walking, almost running, over to the bakery.

7

The toilet was on the top floor, and its small windows overlooked the street, trees, and university's buildings. Its ceilings were low and you had to bend over to get through the door. The ceiling sloped across the room until it almost met the floor. As for the toilet, it stood in the middle like a rectangle cut in the ground by a rock-cutting saw. The hole didn't have a front or back, so the workers could hover over it and do their business while facing either direction – the back of the bathroom wall or the front door, which was kept locked with a bent nail.

To shower at the end of the day they had to stand in one place, under the tap, which hung from the ceiling like a shower head. They went in one after the other, and rarely fought in line, since they usually finished working at different times. Between working and showering they liked to relax a little.

Aarif, the baker, did so by standing up at the front of the bakery, watching the street, or talking to whoever was on the other side of the counter. He didn't look at the female customers until they turned around to leave. When I was there alone, without my father, he talked about their bodies as though he were embracing them, or he lifted his modest tea cup to his lips, took a sip, then licked his lips afterwards, as though he'd just tasted their skin.

The small toilet with the low ceiling was the only one on the block, between the cinema at the top of the street and the restaurant at the bottom. The shoe-shines who sat in front of their boxes by the restaurant would come to the bakery to use the toilet, since the waiters at the restaurant wouldn't allow them near the door because they didn't want the customers to see them. From the bookstore the only person who came was Peter the American, whispering a greeting to everyone he saw. As for the Armenian woman who owned the antique store, and only brushed the back of her hair, she would joke with the workers on her way up the stairs, as though this would distract them from what she was about to do. As soon as the door was closed they'd start making fun of her, but then my father's face would appear, which soon shut them up. He'd wring his hands as if to say: 'What should I do about her?' Then he'd go back to the front counter, and find a way to tell those around him that she couldn't build a bathroom in her shop because it wasn't big enough.

She used to spend her entire day standing on the sidewalk since the shop was filled with broad glass shelves, and there was no room for even a single chair for her to sit on. Even payments were received on the street. To make it seem like she'd chosen a small storefront on purpose, she made sure the store's sign was similarly small, and the only thing she wrote on it was the word 'corner,' in English, as the store itself was on the corner of the street and the church entrance. Elie, who owned an equally diminutive shop full of women's belts, followed suit, and called his one word: 'Elie'. As for our bakery, in which the workers slept and lived, it had an enormous sign the size and width of the front door, on which there were drawings of men and women with their arms outstretched and heads facing up to the heavens, from where a multitude of loaves, Arabic and French breads, rained down. Beneath this illustration, in thick green letters, were the words 'The Greater Bread Company,' to give the impression that the bakery was larger than it actually was, and that it never stopped baking, since its name looked like a long train, with smoke billowing out of it, like that which came from the oven itself.

8

The truth was, we didn't bake or sell French bread. That would have required an oven different from the one we had, smaller, with wide drawers in which the wrapped dough could be placed in the shape of two loops. It resembled compact bedroom cupboards, except that it was made of iron. As for its workers, they had to wear white aprons and gloves so that their hands wouldn't burn from the heat of the drawers.

When the government decreed that the workers in Arabic bakeries had to wear white aprons, my father laughed, as he imagined the workers standing around like patissiers. Soon they'd be inventing dainty metal tongs for them to lift dough with, he scoffed. He believed that bakers' work required a strength that didn't go well with white knee-length aprons, which made everyone look feminine. My aunt's husband, who owned a bakery in Ras Beirut, said that even the owners of bakeries had to wear aprons, and he and my father both laughed, each imagining the other dressed that way. To my uncle, tall and proud, my aunt's husband said that in a white apron he'd look like he had his doctorate.

For my father, a baker was a baker, not what the government deemed he should be; his messy clothes reflected the messy business of manual labour. The bakery itself reflected this too, with its marble step worn thin from years of customers' feet.

That the front counter had an old look, and that its drawers were without locks, with paper bags containing mixtures on the shelf, all meant that the bakery was functioning, and doing well, unlike the other places whose owners spent all their time decorating and fussing over them. He loved seeing the bakery filled to the brim, even if many of those who visited were just people who came to use the bathroom, or people who wanted to use the oven to heat up something of their own. He didn't tell my uncle about them, though, because my uncle turned the shoe-shines away at the door, telling them he had opened a bakery to work not to help other people shit. When the shoe-shines walked off, clutching their cramped bellies, my father would tell my uncle that we wouldn't lose any business by letting people use the loo.

'It's a good deed to those in need,' he'd say.

My uncle would turn away and mutter things under his breath, which my father soon realised were curses, and he'd responded in fancy language: 'Why, how eccentric you are.' So my uncle would go back inside, angry and annoyed, but he wouldn't agree not to keep turning people away if they needed to use the toilet.

Then my father decided to go back to baking with wood, and my uncle stood in front of the pile of large wooden logs and pointed at them, his face turned away as though he had just witnessed a pile of filth. My father said that the gas stove left an aftertaste in the bread, and this shut my uncle up, but he still told our relatives that my father was brainwashed by the college-student customers. On the first day of wood-baking, the workers were done at four instead of one. But the bread tasted much better, my uncle teased.

The bakery kept using the wood a few days a week. But we had to throw the rest of the logs out in the street, because my father couldn't convince his customers that the burnt wooden flints that sometimes flew out of the flame and stuck to the loaves weren't dirt.

But the truth was, the bakery was beginning to hum like a movie theatre when the sound goes out. The workers were going through the motions but weren't actually doing any work. That's what made my father go back to the gas stove, which blared noisily when it burned, as if to encourage and inspire the workers.

9

Mustafa, whose father's bakery wasn't far from ours, crossed the street and went into the stationery store. Probably went there to buy the newspaper, Muhammad said. He came out flipping through a newspaper and hiding his face from us, and Muhammad said this was the second time he'd done this. We stayed on the sidewalk, facing him, waiting, and then he walked over to us, and we started reading it over his shoulder. He'd quickly glance at a page, giving it a cursory look, before reading it thoroughly later once he was alone. But once he noticed we were hanging around, reading over his shoulder, he turned the pages more slowly, even going back to previous pages. Mustafa stopped reading, gave us a look, then asked us if we were planning to read the paper all the way down the street. He tidied its pages and rolled it up, holding it in his hand like a stick.

We walked towards the garden, which we never entered but stood outside, on the sidewalk by its gates. Farhat and Mustafa went ahead of me and Muhammad, talking politics. We overheard them discuss Abdel Nasser, and the Japanese pilots who'd blown themselves up. Muhammad said Ramez was discussing Palestine again, and that he always hung out with people who had money. Mustafa was the shortest of all of us, but he seemed to be the oldest since he never joined in joking around. He also looked older because he shaved his face, and combed his hair in the style of the men whose black-and-white photos hung in barber shops. In his bakery, he would stand alone at the front counter in the afternoons, as though he owned it. He walked ahead of us, watching Farhat wave his hands around, which he loved to do when he spoke. Muhammad said that our friends were talking politics even though neither of them understood a word of what they were saying. Khalil walked a few steps behind us, sometimes catching up with Mustafa to ask if he could borrow the newspaper, then retreating again shyly. He stared at the paper in Mustafa's hand when he got bored of looking at the shops and the building entrances, and the cars passing by. By the time we got to the sidewalk in front of the garden, Khalil had borrowed the paper and was bringing it up close to his eyes.

Muhammad said that those whose minds were small had weak vision. Khalil was staring at the words in the paper as though they were small insects he was afraid would fly away. Muhammad saw that Khalil was practically crashing into those who walked past him, and so he took him by the arm, leading him up the street the way one does a blind man. Khalil gave him a long look, and pulled his arm away, once, twice, until Muhammad's sunken shoulders shook. I angrily told him to leave Khalil alone, but instead, he grabbed his arm with both of his hands. He didn't know what he'd just got himself into, and was terrified to see Khalil's gaze of fermenting anger.

Farhat and Mustafa had walked far ahead of us and were now approaching the crosswalk. I told Muhammad to stop, and went towards him to pull him off Khalil, but he'd already loosened his grip. He was scared, not of Khalil's idiocy, but of his sudden rage, as if it had awoken some truth in his mind.

Khalil continued onwards, trailing us like he wanted to quieten his mind, the mind which no one understood but him. He was walking with his head held up and his hand gripping the newspaper, its pages spread open. I asked Muhammad not to talk to him at all or even look at him for the rest of the day. Muhammad said, his voice shy, that he was only trying to keep him from bumping into people. As we approached the gym, he told me that he wasn't afraid of Khalil's anger but of his strength, which was that of crazy country people.

Khalil didn't want to go into the gym, even though he usually enjoyed watching. He stood alone on the steps of a locked storefront. Mustafa and Farhat took their position in the doorway, and fell silent when Muhammad joined them, listening to what they were saying, while at the same time appearing to make fun of them. Farhat wanted him to get lost, so he told him to go into the gym with me.

'Why don't *you* go?' Muhammad replied, arguing as he always does, itching for a fight.

I refused to go in after hearing them talk like this, and walked a few steps ahead.

Farhat stood with Mustafa, whose entire demeanor was clouded whenever anyone argued or fought. Muhammad followed me, and said that Mustafa liked to stay quiet because when he talked he sounded more idiotic than Khalil. As the trainers left the gym, they blocked the opening of its high and narrow entrance, and took the three steps to the exit without looking down to see what was under their feet. Muhammad said they must spend their entire time at the gym fighting since their bodies were so strong. Then he pointed out how Khalil was balking at them as they walked out of the gym.

'Go and talk to him,' I said, but Muhammad raised his hands, like someone who was good at pushing sadness away.

My brother peeked his head through the door, looking like a real body-builder. When he looked back into the gym to tell Ramez to hurry, his bare forearms showed all sorts of muscles. He smiled at Ramez, and when he saw Muhammad and me he waved at us, raising his bag with the white-rope handle. His hair was still wet and his face was cheerful. Muhammad teasingly asked him how come he was still skinny if he was really lifting weights in there. Ramez charged him, to show off his strength, and Muhammad leaned in to my brother for help, hugging his waist. My brother still managed to appear like he had other things to worry about, and looked at Mustafa and waved while Muhammad hung from his waist.

We stood by the entrance and Ramez said there were too many of us to go to one place, and that we should split up. He hesitated whenever someone suggested somewhere. Mustafa remained silent. We walked together all the way to the end of the wide street. As we prepared to go our separate ways, Khalil, who stood outside our circle, stood still and waited for us to fight over him. As we walked off, Farhat said, 'They think they're better than us.' He swore at them, then Muhammad reminded him of how tight he'd been with Mustafa the entire walk over.

10

The rocks that the bakers call fire rocks, and which they used to make the large kindling fire, would crack loudly in the heat of the flames. Even the ones at the very top of the pile, which the flames and heat can't reach, didn't last longer than six months. They shrunk in size and broke apart like rotten teeth, before falling away. In the cramped space where the flames licked at them, the rocks changed shape and distorted. That narrow space where the bakers worked looked like a wasteland, or a meteor on a scorched planet.

In all Beirut, only one man was strong enough to enter the oven itself: Jamal al-Rishani, whose house was close to Saqia Square. Men congregated around him, hours after the ovens had been turned off, the way men do around a newly dug well. At the bakery, they prepared the oven, in which he could only stand to be in for a couple of minutes. They wiped the rocks with mud so he could stick them quickly in place. 'Let me out,' he'd yell from inside the oven, so that they'd pull out the two boards against which he'd lean his face. The oven remained hot even after it had been shut off for two days. The rocks stayed lit from the inside, even when they were ripped from their places and carried outside, like snakes and reptiles whose bodies stayed alive hours after their death.

On the sidewalk in front of the bakery, the small pile of rocks sat like a recently fallen meteor. They were still red and inflamed even after the workers had dumped several buckets of water over them. The water usually helped a little, but soon the pile would redden again and small pieces of ash would fly off. No one could walk by without stopping in front of the pile and staring. Young female college students would back away from it and ask us what it was. Owners of the block's barbers, stationery stores, and sandwich shops began to come by, leaving their work behind to watch it. We'd all stand around, my father, my aunt's husband, the baker, who was done for the day, and I. When people asked me what it was I told them it was from the oven, but I didn't give any more details so that a sense of mystery remained. As for my father, he gave all sorts of answers, sometimes in sentences so long they became monologues. Occasionally he wailed at passers-by, and at other times he explained to them how the fire ate the heart of the rock itself. The entire time he'd turn his frowning face from the swollen pile to the passer-by.

My father didn't let a single instance like this pass without taking advantage of the opportunity to lecture people for hours. On normal opening days he told stories about working at bakeries, stories that were obviously made up, because they were always different the second time round.

When a woman asked him why he hadn't installed an air conditioner in the bakery he told her his version of science: that cold air and warm air were separate entities and it was impossible to join the two. He attempted this brand of science on the university professors, telling them that the two different temperatures would hurt the dough and keep the yeast from rising. As for the cookie dough, he claimed that the foreign bakers (who wanted to manufacture it in large quantities) came, observed, and left defeated, not having understood a single thing about how it worked.

He used his hands to better illustrate his theories about hot and cold air. He made hot air look like clouds that bumped into the oven, like against a force field, crashing into the cold air, which he also illustrated with his hands, descending from the air vents. If he failed at explaining something, it was simply because it was inexplicable. He made such things appear even more impenetrable so that his ignorance about them would remain a secret.

In answer to the university professors who told him that the cookie dough's yeast rose according to the temperature and moisture levels that surrounded it, he said that the scent of a female customer's perfume could ruin it. If they agreed with him, he'd tell them that certain kinds of perfume ruined it, and others didn't.

He took advantage of every opportunity to show those on the outside what happened inside our bakery. On our street, the bankers and the store-owners kept the same hours, so they came by the store at the same time. The store-owners did nothing but undo buttons on shirts for their customers to try on, or dust books to sell. The barber, who spent most of his time playing the oud, never ceased to be amazed by our bakery. He loved seeing the large amounts of bread on boards, and the old man who transferred the 100-kilo bags of flour on his back. He stood staring, his hands on his hips, then approached my father to say, 'What is all this, neighbour? My God.' The store-owners of the street liked to eat one or two of the small sandwiches that shrank when they were heated up, on the sidewalk in front of the bakery. Their stores were simply rooms; inside there wasn't enough room to make anything. My father said he could greet them one by one as he walked up the street, because their faces were clear behind the store windows. According to my uncle, who delivered the bread in his car, they knew nothing about the Beirut in which they had grown up. He said that one of the brothers who owned the sandwich shop once asked him for directions back to his own shop. My uncle gave him a lift, and he said that when he dropped the man off, he got out of the car with a look of exhaustion, as though he'd just gone on a long journey.

Bakeries exhaust their workers but strengthen their bodies. The Armenian woman who never brushed the back of her hair stood outside her shop and stared as my brother ordered several drinks from the juice shop. When he saw her behind him, watching him drink, he noticed that she was counting each cup he gulped down.

She told him his health was a blessing he should cherish, and he replied that he knew, and turned around quickly, back to the bakery where he was expected.

The pile of rubble that came from inside the oven was part of our work. My father looked at it as if to say he knew that this was what fire did to rocks, and that rocks reacted this way to being lit for long periods of time. I stood near it the way I stood in the small alleyway by the church.

I didn't see either of the sisters who usually came in to buy four loaves of bread, but I found out where their house was. Passers-by and customers greeted me the way people greet someone they aren't expecting to see, and they invited me to their homes, and I greeted them and smiled and stood in my usual pose, not moving. When a girl finally came to talk to me, I responded as though I were much older, even though she was five or ten years my senior.

11

Instead of singing with Muhammad El-Halaby, I began to recite poetry. I don't mean the poems they made you learn at school, the ones that children read out, repeat, and memorise with their parents, but ones I found by myself, in books of older students or from the end of my own book, the part the teacher hadn't got to yet.

Muhammad El-Halaby sat on an office chair, and I sat on a pile of extra bags that were still tied with rope, so I could stay close to the cash drawer, which my father said no one else was allowed to open. I would recite a poem, which I had memorised by heart, even though my teacher had only asked us to memorise parts of it, or one from which Abdel Halim sang just a few verses, or a poem our teacher had cut from a journal.

Muhammad El-Halaby listened to my recitations, sighing like singers do. 'Mmm,' he'd murmured, pursing his lips when I raised my voice or otherwise appeared enthusiastic about a verse. I said, 'O night,' at the end of a verse and he thought it was the end of the entire poem. He went back to listening when I began a new section, nodding his head like someone in deep thought, as he waited for his turn to sing.

He always found a way to take his turn. Humming a tune as soon as I stopped reciting, under the pretence that he was warming up his voice, or starting to sing right after I stopped, as though my recitation was the opening act for his song. He wasn't just good at singing, he also knew how to use his voice. A woman came in and asked him to keep singing, and he did so loudly for a short while as if to appease her. After she applauded him, he'd answer her the way professional singers do: 'Thank you, thank you so much,' or he'd raise his arms then cover his belly and say, 'It is the listener who should be applauded.'

Then he'd go behind the counter to the bread, which was covered with large nylon cloths, to get her order. I stayed behind with the customer, to whom he always assumed that I spoke in his absence. 'What did you say to her?' he'd ask, as soon as she walked off with her bread, and I'd tell him I barely had enough time to say anything at all. Or I'd say that I wasn't interested in that particular customer, but in her friend who sometimes came in with her. In order to push me into talking to them, he asked one of the sisters who lived by the church to come in and choose the bread herself. Then he motioned to me and nodded his head twice in her direction as if to say, 'Go, go.' I lost my voice when I stood next to her, and I knew I wouldn't get it back unless I raised it, pretending we were talking amongst a bunch of other people.

'Did the Jordanian family that was renting a house in your neighbourhood move?' I asked, and then told her that the restaurant by the church was about to get a new name, since their sign had been torn down. I didn't look at her feet, which were exposed in open sandals, until she went off with her four loaves of bread. I told Muhammad El-Halaby that she was prettier than her sister today, the tall, thin one who sounded like she was laughing whenever she talked.

But then I became confused and couldn't choose between them. They took turns each day to come in for the four loaves of bread. While they looked different in height and build, their beauty was equal, so that they resembled twins. I fell for the first one until the second showed up, and I told Muhammad El-Halaby that I was sure it was her. 'Did you talk to her?' he asked, and I told him that her laughing voice made it difficult for me to say anything, and that if she really wanted me to do so, she would have quietened it down.

It wasn't just the sisters; there was a blonde with little pimples, and a redhead who came in to use the phone. El-Halaby got off the chair and let her sit on it in the hope that she'd stay longer. After she left, I picked up the telephone and put the receiver to my ear to entertain him, but, secretly, I felt as though I'd touched her. Finally, there was the Indian woman who thought I was singing when I was actually reciting verses on top of the flour bags.

'Is that a Lebanese song?' she asked in English, and I answered her, also in English, that it was a poem.

12

Ramez's older brothers, who are about my father's age, said that he was bad with money and should never have any of his own. Their wives, who hated washing their husbands' clothes, said that money would ruin him, and that he would spend it all on whores in the public market. Ramez used to go to the market, but only to the sandwich shop at the market's entrance. He'd only been inside the actual market once or twice, and left it in a hurry, terrified that someone would catch him. But he saw the prostitutes flaunting their bodies behind the glass the way merchants do with their wares. He said they were ugly, and that the beautiful ones, the ones who charged twenty liras, were in the rooms of the apartments above, where the rooms were separated and hidden from public view.

Even when he went over to their house for dinner, he did nothing to disprove what his brothers and their wives thought of him, and appeared incapable of taking care of himself. Before his death, his father had asked Ramez several times if he needed anything, and Ramez said he would take whatever he was given. One of his brothers said they weren't talking about his allowance then, but about his share in their father's inheritance. Ramez grew silent at that. As they began to count out his part of the inheritance, he lifted his head and looked past the open door, to see if anyone was coming by. They offered him the land in the valley, but he didn't want it.

Neither did he want the four-bedroom house in Deia, nor the land in Khalla, which came with 3,000 liras. Their brother who lived in Masyataba said that Ramez must have wanted only cash. So, they asked him if he wanted his share in cash, and he nodded his head and said he didn't want any land, nor did he want to live in a house in Deia.

His father couldn't convince him to take the property, and Ramez couldn't persuade any of them that he wanted the money to buy himself a bakery. He told us in the Fiat's rearview mirror that his brothers' wives eavesdropped on their conversation from behind the door, and that they ran to their rooms and told each other that he wanted the money to spend on his 'organ'. Muhammad said they must have known this because they were the ones who washed his dirty underwear. Farhat was more serious, and said that they were ripping Ramez off, and would keep his money for themselves, never letting him be more than an employee, and so making even more money off him.

But Ramez felt rich with the 10,500 liras his brothers kept for him and the forty liras they paid him for his monthly services at the butcher's. In the Fiat, the garden, or at our house, where we stretched out on the couches, we'd tease him that he was being exploited, and he'd reply that he'd sue his brothers and their wives. He forgot his anger when we asked him what he'd do with the 10,500 liras, and he said that he'd go to Egypt with it, but before that, he'd spend the night with a woman at the hotel we saw in the mountains.

At the end of the month we all went to the butcher shop to collect the rent Ramez was owed. It looked old and didn't have a storefront. If all the butchers packed up their meats and left, it would have resembled any old grocery and no one would have guessed that it was once a butcher shop. We passed by its entrance's tall doors and waited for Ramez to come out with the forty liras, preparing ourselves for the possibility that he wouldn't get them. Muhammad said if that happened we should attack the meats in the market and devour them. The idea of that made Khalil laugh.

Ramez peered out at us over the doors and motioned for us to wait. When the pretty woman came out carrying a bag of meat, we knew that the butcher would finally be able to listen to what Ramez had to say. Farhat paced in front of the entrance, watching the man listen to Ramez, a huge knife buried in the wooden block in front of him. Muhammad jokingly said that the man would cut Ramez up, then we finally saw him leave the store. He said nothing, but we knew from his smile and his swift walk that the forty liras was in his pocket, folded, crumpled, and rotten with blood and the smell of meat.

13

On the inside, bakeries differ much more than houses do. In Mustafa's bakery, the oven was flipped, and faced west, the same direction as the bakers, so that they took the same steps forward as they did back. Also, the normally short step on which bakers stand was really high, making them look like they were working on another floor entirely. In my uncle's bakery, the bathroom was on the bottom floor, which made the whole place smell different. My uncle going in to talk to his bakers would put on a serious face, as though he were a stranger in his own bakery. Ramez, too, made a face when he went through the tall doors at his brother's bakery.

Counting up all the bakeries in Ras Beirut, bakers always forgot the one that had neither storefront nor counter, its customers buying their bread from the sidewalk. Space in the back room was tight too, and the doors to the stove and the oven looked like one, the wall around them dark and burnt. They were still able to store several worthless items in that tight space: empty boxes of yeast, large, discarded oil cans, old sponges used to wipe the loaves of bread, and bags of cheesecloth they'd squeezed dough out of. No one throws anything out at a bakery, except for dust-coloured dough, old cigarettes, brewed tea leaves from the bottom of the pot, and leftovers. Every three or four months, my uncle would stand in the middle of the bakery and stare at all the useless stuff and wonder aloud why we kept it all. Then he'd chuck all the empty boxes into the fire, and gather up all the used oil cans for people to buy and reuse, or even take for free. Finally, he'd throw everything else out into the large garbage pail. If he was feeling inspired, he'd even clean under the tables and in the storage space. He would open up bags and frown at their contents; hold up pieces of fabric and ask those around him, 'Whose shirt is this?' or 'Whose trash is this?' Then he'd move the things away from him as though they were contagious and say, 'Into the pail, into the pail.'

Each bakery differed from the others on the inside, in its appearance and in the strange ways the lofts and scaffolds and ovens were set up. Those workers who moved around and worked in different bakeries knew all too well the despair that struck one who worked at a bakery that was not his own. They'd speak to him soothingly like they were long-lost relatives, peering in on him through doors and small windows and offering him drinks and cigarettes, behaving like house servants who entertain their friends when the masters are out. For the most part, all this occurred when the bakery owners were busy chatting up customers. This suited my father just fine. He only went to other bakeries to pick up a previous worker he couldn't find a replacement for. 'Tell him you won't be back tomorrow,' he'd whisper, and if the worker loudly offered my father tea, he knew that the worker would be at our bakery the very next day.

14

The cutting machine looked miniscule in the back of the truck that delivered it to the bakery. Before he bought it, my father talked about how popular it was, and so by the time the truck had reached our bakery I thought it had already distributed the machine to every single bakery in town. All we had to do to fit it on the counter was move the slab of marble on which the cutter took in the dough. Ghaleb, the cutter, hung around the bakery to learn how to use it. He said it looked like a small bed with a pillow floating above. The salesman who brought it used the dough that was left over from the last batch to try it out. He lowered a loaf into the top opening, and it came out stretched, then round out of the next opening, which had a white, flour-hued piece of cloth at the end of it. Ghaleb was rounding out the bread with two strikes. 'It is even faster than him,' said the salesman, as he imitated Ghaleb's hand movements but speeding up to show just how fast the machine was going.

On Ghaleb's turn to try, he seemed confused and slow as though he'd never worked with bread before. The loaves came out stretched from the lower hole, and my father picked them up and balled them up so Ghaleb could have another go. My father noticed that the salesman was staring at Ghaleb's fingers, and said, 'You have to use your fingers with this thing, not your palms.' Doing this, his hands seemed long and webbed. Muhammad El-Halaby, whose speech was as beautiful as his song, said that the machine grabbed the dough from him. The salesman agreed, and told Ghaleb to move closer to it.

Ghaleb left a few days after the machine's arrival; not because my uncle got angry with him when he saw the loaves of bread stretched out like boards, but because he hated working with machines. He told my father that a little boy would be able to take his place, and probably do a better job. Those few days after the machine's arrival, he felt alienated from the trio he was part of, forced to join the ranks of the workers and the delivery men. My father tried to convince him that the machine would make work easier for him, but he said he was tired of the forceful sound it made whenever it ejected a loaf. He knew that my father wouldn't return the machine. It was true that the bread it made was less round, but it worked much faster than a worker ever could.

When Ghaleb left, my father said that he hadn't known what to do with his body in front of the machine, and that a man like him couldn't work on a machine that was so easily held and contained. It wasn't like the dough machine, which weighed a ton and could fit 100 kilos of dough. He said this in front of Nawwaf the dough-maker, so that he and Hussein, who were the remaining members of the stone-table trio, wouldn't leave us, or leave their friend Ghaleb behind, whose company they enjoyed – even if it was true that he didn't talk much.

15

Muhammad El-Halaby enjoyed working on the cutter, since it brought him closer to the workers and helped him become one of them. He no longer spent his day jumping between the boards and the scaffolds, or keeping up with the bakers. From his very first day on the machine he brought the bread out round, and was so fast he almost needed two transferers. My father would tell him through the window that looked onto the workers to flatten the dough, and Muhammad knew the exact thickness needed. He also learned quickly how to work the grips that widen and narrow the distance between the blades.

His work on the machine gave him a fluency that would help him make the transition to the kind of life he wanted. He had thought that his singing among the workers, day after day, meant he was stuck with them. One of the bakers had become used to his voice and teasingly told him he should stand in front of the radio station and sing until the station's boss came out and heard him. The other workers also began to joke, about how some throats were so ruined by cigarette smoke that the only thing that could save them was the *kishk* flour which they used to clean their throats with. He would join them in the joke, but always from the position of someone who was a singer. So he would tell them they should put a slab of lard on their throats before the flour to clean out the throat and soften it up. But then it was as though he was making fun of himself, because his joke made it seem like he did this himself or at least thought about it.

Standing at the machine and singing, he would face the wall, to give the impression that he was entertaining himself, not those around him. The workers who stayed after Ghaleb left would listen to Muhammad sing while they worked. They didn't tease him, the way those near the oven had. Sometimes they would whisper 'How lovely,' and he knew then that they too had found a way to pass the time.

'Sing, Muhammad,' the baker who stood before the oven would say. Once the sound of the bakery was louder than the singing, he would turn to the boy who was putting the loaves out and say, 'Sing boy, sing.' The boy would blush, knowing that the baker was teasing him, and the baker would laugh. Sometimes he would persist and bait the boy further, throwing loaves of hot bread at him. He wouldn't stop until he heard my father come in and tell him to leave the kid alone.

16

Khalil began working at our bakery when his father told him that being unemployed in Beirut would be the end of him. Ramez laughed in the Fiat's rearview, then turned his head to face us and made us laugh too. Muhammad, who was sitting next to him, began to imitate Khalil and imagine what he would be like with a grown man's voice. Ramez said that we were yet to be ruined, and admitted that he still hadn't done anything at the public market. Muhammad told Ramez that he was already ruined, and was a coward who liked to stare at women from afar but was too afraid to be alone with them in a room. '*I'm* a coward?' Ramez said, and Farhat chimed in from the backseat that he would sleep with a woman if we paid for him. Ramez kept staring at Khalil in the rearview, as if to determine whether he knew anything about women. We talked about what we'd do to them if we ever got lucky enough to have any, and Ramez raised an eyebrow, studying the way Khalil leaned into the window. He saw him staring off into the distance and letting the wind play with his hair, eyes half-shut. 'I bet he's listening, I bet he understands,' Ramez said. 'Why else would he be so quiet?'

They used to follow him to the fancy Western-style bathroom at my house, where he liked to stand. He would just stand there, looking at the toilet and the sink, running his palm over the long bathtub's white porcelain surface. 'He must be imagining a naked woman in it,' Ramez would say. Farhat disagreed; he thought Khalil imagined himself in the bathtub, naked, staring down at his erection rising above the water. Khalil never closed the door if he went to that bathroom, or when he pissed in the Arabic one. Ramez wanted to make sure we knew he went into the rooms in the public market, so he told us that he would take Khalil with him next time and make him try it out.

My father told the bakery workers that Khalil was a relative of ours so that they would stop making fun of him. Khalil would stand in the doorway between the counter and the back room and wait for the customers to show up. To signal their arrival he'd move his head and body forward, and then wait for my father to tell him what to do. 'Four loaves, Khalil,' my father would say, lifting the requisite number of fingers. Khalil would come back with the loaves stacked in his hand, and my father would say, 'Good work, Khalil,' to let the customers know that Khalil moved measuredly because he was slow in the head. Every time he brought the loaves he looked like someone who had accomplished a major task. But he didn't rest afterwards; he went back to his spot in the doorway, and waited. My father noticed that standing this way tired him out more than work did, but he didn't teach him to relax because he worried that Khalil would take it as an insult and never come back. 'He's a relative of ours,' my father told my uncle, who sneered when he saw Khalil's head hovering at the counter. Sometimes my uncle bumped into him on purpose on his way into the bakery, in an attempt to move him into the back room. One day, my aunt's husband came to visit, and stood out on the sidewalk, and my uncle complained to him that my father let Khalil work there and even paid him for it. My aunt's husband suggested that my uncle take him on deliveries, and he nodded as if to say, 'Ha! That's the last thing I need.'

Through his facial and bodily movements my uncle was able to tell those around him everything he felt. If he flicked his hand as though to slide something over, it meant that he was only at the bakery for a short while; if he winked and raised his eyebrow, it implied that my father's idiotic nature was irreversible; parting his lips but keeping his teeth together, then quickly nodding his head twice, showed that he was so angry he could die, but that there was nothing he could do about it; and when he threw the bags of bread violently into the back of the delivery truck, or if he didn't answer people's questions, or pushed a bakery worker out of his way, it was because he knew that my father was staring at him, and that, in a few minutes, he would say, 'Why, how eccentric you are,' the only words he pronounced in standard Arabic, without any gestures. Words he directed only at him.

Khalil took my uncle pushing him into the back room as a personal blow. He looked at my father to ask whether it would lead to a brawl, and my father in turn stared at my uncle with unblinking eyes. Afterwards, he went to Khalil. 'You can stay at our house tonight,' he'd say, and, a couple of customers later, again would say, 'You can stay at our house tonight,' to let him know that he hadn't changed his mind.

17

My father had a medical book which included things even students of medicine didn't know. It was huge, the size of a dictionary, even though it had lost some pages from the front and back. He bought it secondhand, looking like an antique, from the paper-bill seller (whose motorcycle storage box fitted plenty of books). My father made it appear even more ancient from carrying it around and flipping through it. Except for the *Qu'ran*, which he read when he was a child, he never owned or read another book. He used to carry it by its spine, that part of it that was fortified with thread and glue. Then he began to carry it in a bag from the bakery, until that tore, or lost its handles. If a page fell out, he'd replace it without worrying too much whether it was in the right order. The order wasn't that important since the book wasn't a novel; each page was filled with diseases and descriptions. It was possible that when a page ripped out, it helped him place it better: for example, it was easier to find the entry for jaundice if he placed it loosely in the middle of the book instead of having to turn the pages left and right until he found it. In addition, the ripped pages became like bookmarks for the sections that came before and after.

My uncle would stand on the sidewalk and point his thumb in the direction of my father, who held the book up and read it, and say to my aunt's husband or to anyone who would listen, 'Look, he's studying for his exams,' or that the doctors who came by the bakery were ruining him by indulging him when he talked about medicine. There was one doctor, a gastroenterologist, who listened to my father in wonder, then asked him how he knew all this, even though he saw the medical book on the shelf. And when my father described all the cures for jaundice, the doctor nodded his head, as though really thinking about what my father had said, and replied, 'Interesting, we should try that.' My father also talked to this doctor about diseases completely unrelated to gastrointestinal ones, because, according to him, every part of the body was related. Talking to my aunt's husband about this, he gave him his own point of view and the doctor's as well, then compared them in a defiant tone.

He discussed bodies like they were being dissected right in front of him, and described how food reached the intestines and from there travelled to the bowels' door. He would think about his old science lessons and knew that his descriptions were correct, and that the work our body did was easier than the commentary we attached to it. The difficult part of science was the naming and memorising of things. But my father remembered it all even though some of the plants were as old as the medical book itself.

It was the plants and herbs volume that was the thickest, full of chemicals, not just classifications. He went to help care for my aunt's knees, having filled the delivery van's trunk with two days' worth of cloth. My aunt let him wrap the plant-filled cloths around her legs, and when he changed them everyday he told her the yellow liquid that was dripping from them was the rejected illness, oozing out of her body. She said that she was feeling better even though she was walking crookedly, her knees puffy from the cloths wrapped around them. My mother saw that she was becoming weaker, so she told my father to take her to a doctor, and that he couldn't take on such a large responsibility.

Instead, he told stories about people he had healed. He always began these by saying that people came to him after they'd become disillusioned with the doctors who'd lied to them and taken their money. According to my father, many of the people we saw every day had been patients he had helped, but no longer worked with since they refused to acknowledge that their recovery was thanks to him, and not to the hospital's doctors and nurses. To Michel, the barber (who insisted on calling himself Mike, despite his old age) he said that he refused to heal his eyes, since they were very sensitive parts of the body. But he was lying; he thought Michel was selfish. After my father had cured him of his backache, Michel began going for strolls on the sidewalk as though he wasn't through testing his body for more damage. He never came into our bakery to thank my father on these strolls. All he said to my father was, 'I've gotten better, neighbour,' as though he'd healed himself unaided by anyone else.

So my father let him suffer with his eye disease. Whenever he looked at anyone, they'd water so much he'd have to shut them. Soon, they flooded so badly he could barely see his customers as they walked into his barber shop, and he came begging for my father's help, but to no avail. Each time he told this story, my father wanted to put the listeners in Michel's place, and have them pleading for more. No one ever told him to change his mind about helping because they were all busy trying to look as though they believed every word he said.

18

When the younger sister came by the bakery, she seemed more beautiful than her older sister ... but when the older sister came by, she seemed more beautiful than her younger sister. Muhammad would leave me with either of them, taking bread into the back room if we stayed in the front, or going out to the front if we went to the back room. 'Did you say anything to her?' he'd ask me, and I'd say I didn't but that she knew I liked her because of the way I slowly prepared her order, and the way I counted the bread, twice. The sisters were equally beautiful even though one was taller than the other. The short one's feet, which she flaunted in her open sandals, were just as beautiful as the tall one's knees. When one of them left the bakery, I told Muhammad that she was the more beautiful and that I was smart not to have talked to her sister the day before. That way if she'd gone home and told her sister, I wouldn't know how to act around her when she came back the following day.

As soon as she was out the bakery door I couldn't wait for the day after tomorrow, when she'd come back again. But then, at around four o'clock, I'd forget all about her because I was busy thinking about the girl who tied all her hair up, or about the girl who heard me recite a poem from my flour bag seat, or about the two girls who came in to ask, in English, for directions to a building at the university.

The girls who visited our bakery were more beautiful than the ones who went to other bakeries. There were only three or four beauties that visited Ramez's bakery, in the same way that there are only that many beautiful girls in every neighbourhood. The girls at our bakery were stunning because they knew how to flaunt their single attractive quality. If the girl who tied her hair up lived in Ramez's neighbourhood, she probably wouldn't have been considered one of the local beauties, but here she was.

The girls of our bakery would be like any other girls if we washed them and hung them up to dry. But we didn't, and it helped that we had no idea what their houses, in which they made themselves beautiful, looked like. They found a single quality to flaunt, or sometimes none at all. The American woman who drove by in her sporty two-seater Jaguar left one of her high heels on the car's floor-mat and one on the seat, as though she'd spent the evening partying in her car, and went directly from it to her bedroom. My brother and I would stand and admire the car: we'd stare at the tiny leather heel and wonder how something so small could carry a whole woman. We imagined her naked foot walking in the heel, and I told my brother her husband must have parked and left in a hurry, forgetting to pick the shoe up and take it inside. But my brother thought they did everything on purpose, and he said that her husband meant to leave the shoe out, just as he meant to leave the car in a hurry, parked in the street on which there were no other cars like it. Sometimes my brother said we should turn our backs to the car so the man wouldn't get the pleasure of seeing us admiring it.

The woman, whose hair was soft and cut above the neck, had a head that looked like the front of the car, ready for a race. Unlike everyone else who'd tripped or fallen out of a tree when they were children, she didn't have a single scratch on her face. She had the face and body of a doll, but a pregnant one, with a puffed out stomach, and wore a wide house dress, except it was made of material for use outdoors. My brother said she would probably miscarry the baby in her belly because her body wasn't strong enough for childbirth. We asked the bookstore employee what she did at the store and he said she just talked to everyone, and that she was as sweet as she looked.

He meant that she was a doll.

The bookstore was like a university, and everyone spent their time there having big discussions. The girls liked to be talked to, and even laughed along. The bookstore employee lectured us, saying that the key to talking to the girls wasn't courage, but simply acting like you already knew them. To demonstrate, he didn't just talk to the girls when they came out of the store, but also picked up and flipped the pages of the books they had in their arms. I stood by my brother and watched, excitedly awaiting one of the sisters. But when afternoon came, I found his advice difficult to follow. I did nothing but count the loaves slowly and walked out of the back room with her, as if what I had to say was too large for small talk.

19

The person who helped my father the most during his medical stint was Abu Qassem, a bald man who lived in our neighbourhood. He came by the bakery more often after my father began to read aloud to him his favourite entries in the medical book. Abu Qassem would sit in a chair and put his upturned palms under his legs as if trying to lift his body up. 'Hello baldie,' my uncle would say on his way back from deliveries. 'Hello, dummy,' Abu Qassem would reply. My uncle would jokingly kick him out of the bakery, or tell him in a serious tone that bakeries are places of work, not cafés where people drink liquor and talk for hours.

Abu Qassem travelled between all the bakeries in Ras Beirut, delivering gossip from one to the other. 'Where does Abu Mustafa get his *za'atar*?' he asked, and said the smell of it was so delicious it wafted all through the bakery the moment they brought it out of the oven. My father hated that Abu Mustafa's *za'atar* bread was better than ours, but he liked it when people described it that way – with its smell filling the bakery.

After he took the second bite out of the *za'atar* bread we gave him, and on which we'd sprinkled an extra dash of sumac, my father asked, 'So, is Abu Mustafa's still better?' Abu Qassem shook his head, as though he'd just tasted something he'd never experienced at our bakery before. When he took the final bite, he looked around for a place to toss the wrapper, and my uncle asked him how many visitors the bakery had today. What my uncle really meant was, 'How many *za'atar* breads have you had here for free today?' Abu Qassem fished in his pocket for a quarter lira. My uncle didn't prevent him from paying, so Abu Qassem brought out a bare hand and looked at my uncle as though to say that the hair on a pig's ass was better than him.

Abu Qassem didn't just deliver gossip between bakery owners, but their employees too. Once my uncle went out on deliveries and my father got busy with customers, he walked over to the employees and told them what they liked to hear. He told the baker who listened while he worked that the other bakery owners paid their bakers by the flour bag, not by the day. Then he made his way to the stove workers, and told them about the boxers that made money in fights but spent it all on women who took more than cash, because they weakened their bodies too. All except Ali Ghandoor, who was too stupid to spend money on himself because he believed it when the contractors told him that the fights didn't make any money. After one of the fights he stood on the sidewalk outside the gym as he didn't have anywhere else to go. Ali Ghandoor was just so helpless, and if it weren't for Abu Qassem, he would have spent the night without food or shelter. He was nothing like the singer Fahd Ballan, who (despite the fact that like Ali, he, too, was a bakery worker) had women throwing themselves in front of his car, totally fearless of their lives.

Abu Qassem listed off the names of singers and fighters and said that they were all bakery workers too. He said that most of them admitted to it, and the ones who didn't had something in them that gave it away. Like Fahd Ballan, whose fists were the size of two regular ones because of all the years he spent breaking dough and rolling it out. Ghaleb asked him if he had ever shaken his hand himself, and Abu Qassem opened his own hand to show how small his palm was in Fahd Ballan's. When my father called to him from the front room, he went out and instantly took up the medical talk that the customers had interrupted. 'Arabic medicine heals cancer,' he told my father, and related a story about a man who was covered in spots and tried everything to heal them until a Bedouin woman made him sit with goats and eat what they ate for ten days, at the end of which his body was completely healed. He told my father the man lived in his village, and that he could visit him whenever he liked.

My father didn't have disdain for Abu Qassem the way he did for the university doctors and professors. Each time Abu Qassem left my father felt he'd learned something new from him, as though he'd spent time with a book. He enjoyed memorising Abu Qassem's descriptions, as well as those he heard from the bag sellers, flour carriers, old bakery workers, and the other men who visited the bakery. He loved the strange descriptions, the ones his mind accepted after some thought. My father decided, for example, that it was better to eat what goats ate than what cows or sheep did: plants which are higher up on trees. Since the Bedouin woman prescribed the goat's food without knowing that higher plants are better than the others, my father decided that doctors should know this too, and well enough to be tested on it.

20

In order for them to study at night and sleep during the day, Farhat and Muhammad pitched a tent on the roof of Farhat's building. His was at least two or three storeys higher than the buildings that surrounded it. But his parents refused to let him do this until he explained to them that studying meant pacing, and that he couldn't very well keep the lights on all night over the sleeping heads of his siblings, or pace back and forth between their sleeping bodies. He said the only thing this would cost them was the sofa in the dining room, which he would return anyway, right after he passed his exams. Farhat placed two shutters in the corner of the roof. Usually the residents piled their shutters up in the storage space because they took up too much room in the apartments when they were opened. Muhammad brought a straw mat from his house and hung it up on the clotheslines. They both put up an electric wire with three dangling light bulbs, under which they could pace up and down.

Muhammad knew he was supposed to be completely silent while going up the steps to Farhat's apartment. He was also aware that his voice made him sound like someone pretending to be polite when he asked if Farhat was free to go up and study. Farhat's mother would tell him not to mess around on the roof and to get serious about studying, as though she sensed the unintended impoliteness of his tone. Muhammad began to lower his head and crouch when he passed by their door, in an attempt to hide his shadow, or he stayed away from the stair banister and quickly took the ladder up to the roof. As for Ramez, he switched shifts and began working nights at the bakery so he could spend his days visiting them, and he would run up the stairs even at dawn when the whole building was asleep.

Ramez would arrive, out of breath from running, to find them both asleep on the narrow couch, the books, which had fallen from their grips, spread out on the floor. He made an art out of waking them: he would stand a few steps away from the tent, take out a loaf of *za'atar* bread, and bring it slowly to Farhat's mouth, as if to hand-feed him; or, he picked one of the books off the ground and lifted it in front of Muhammad's face then blew into his ear to wake him; or he placed his head between theirs and talked to them in a feminine voice, because he knew they were dreaming of women. He even stuck a key in one of their cheeks and turned it as if it was in the ignition of a car.

That time, Muhammad woke up and asked him if he had brought the car. Farhat just stared at Ramez's face, then at the face of his watch, and turned to look at the crack in the corner between the doors. At 5.30am, the couple that couldn't have kids began fooling around in bed, until about 5.45am, when they realised that they were being watched. Farhat saw the husband go to the window and shut it, and said, 'They've noticed,' ducking his head. He looked up again, and although the window was now closed, he knew which other ones to look through. At that time of the morning, there was enough light outdoors to illuminate the belly buttons and bare legs of the women who were too warm through the night to cover up, not just in that building but in the ones around it too. Muhammad spied at them from the opposite end of the roof, until Farhat said something and he ran over to make sure that Farhat didn't keep the view to himself.

'Where is she? Where?' Muhammad put his head over Farhat's. They faced the same direction until Ramez took Muhammad's place.

Together they watched the bare-legged beauties whose underwear rode up in their sleep, or who slept on their tummies with their rear ends high, or whose bare arms reached down to the corners of their belly buttons. After it got really hot outside, the couple opened their window again and resumed their flip-flopping in bed, but they kept their underwear on until the very end, when they closed it again. If it was too hot the window stayed open, and they'd hide in the corner of the room, far away from the bed.

Ramez never brought the car for them to go out in at night. His brother kept taking it right after he fell asleep. Muhammad asked if he brought it when he saw the keys after he woke up, and Ramez laughed, saying he didn't bring it on purpose so they wouldn't be distracted from their studies. He laughed some more to let them know he didn't think they were made for studying, and Farhat angrily said they didn't need his car. But Ramez turned to Muhammad and made a gesture with his hands to indicate the movement Muhammad would soon have to make as an undergarment seller at the entrance of the market.

Ramez thought this would be the perfect job for Muhammad because when he talked his hands seemed to be opening boxes and pulling out pairs of underwear to drape in front of customers' eyes; customers who would then buy the underwear not for their material or colour, but because Muhammad's hands were so convincing.

The roof tent didn't help Farhat's studies but only furthered his hunger for women. He began to know them individually and watched them carefully one by one. In the afternoons Farhat's classmates would come to the roof, and other students as well, some of whom had taken eighty or more exams in four consecutive years. The conversations would turn from the subject of forthcoming competitions to remembering the answers which one of the teachers had leaked. Sometimes they'd talk about which students passed last year and who failed, and who got their certificates in Egypt ... Egypt, where girls came over to students' apartments and spent the whole night.

21

Once Radwan, Muhammad El-Halaby's brother, showed up, the singing in the back room doubled and undulated. 'They're like two speakers of a radio,' my brother said, because he hated listening to that type of music. Muhammad stood in front of the machine and started a song, with his brother joining in. Their voices started off soft, as though deliberating which song to sing. After one voice became louder, the other followed, providing the backing vocals and harmonies.

Hearing Radwan singing on his own, the baker encouraged him to do so more often. My father disagreed and thought Muhammad El-Halaby had a better voice, because his brother's throat was still young and undeveloped. Also, he was more focused, and didn't get too self-indulgent with the songs. He pronounced half a word then swallowed the other half, shaking his head left and right, so it looked like he was singing one song while his head sang another.

Radwan liked to play about as much as sing. He would walk off from the shelves and stand by the door to the front room if a girl walked in, and spy on her, while hiding from my father. Soon, the baker would yell at him to get back to work, and my father would see him staring at the girl. My father would yell at him also, calling him a boy, making sure that the girl knew that this immature person was checking her out. All of this entertained the workers, but eventually my father approached Radwan and told him that if he wanted to keep working there he had to stay focused.

Even so, the female customers began to notice Radwan because of his singing. He raised his voice in their direction to let them know he sang only for them. The baker teased him, saying they'd bring him chocolates and candy the next day because they thought he was a little kid. Then he asked him what he would do with them if they ever took him home. My father heard this and warned the baker, telling him not to talk that way to Radwan and ruin him. The baker replied that he himself would be ruined if that little devil kept working by him.

He never tired of playing, even when the workers had finished and gone home, and would hang out in the front room barefoot, walking all around its edges as if in search of some hidden thing. With no one to talk to, he bugged Khalil, who stood between the front and back rooms, and asked him if he saw the mouse that had just run past. Khalil looked at the lines in the dusty tiles that Radwan made with his toe, lines that were supposed to be the mouse's tracks. Radwan grabbed Khalil and tried to show him the garbage pail, but Khalil didn't move at all, and Muhammad El-Halaby told Radwan to leave him alone. 'They'll fire us if you don't stop,' he told Radwan when they went to the back to eat their lunch.

His brother's arrival changed Muhammad El-Halaby, who stayed in the back room all afternoon and didn't change out of his work clothes until he was certain he was done for the day. He told his brother to eat from the large pot all the workers ate their dinners out of. If Radwan played with his food, putting an entire boiled egg in his mouth, Muhammad El-Halaby got annoyed and slapped him twice on the head, hard enough to almost choke him on the egg.

But even when he moved around rapidly and angrily, Muhammad El-Halaby could not hide his playful nature. 'Come here,' he tells his brother when he sees him carrying a kilo of iron to slam on the ground. 'Put the kilo down, put it on the table, put it down,' he tells

Radwan, while Muhammad El-Halaby approaches him slowly, as if to unhand him of a weapon that might go off and hit something.

Radwan goes back to teasing Khalil, even before his tears of anger have dried. He lowers his hand towards Khalil's crotch and snaps his fingers, as if trying to entice a cat to play. His brother says nothing because he knows Radwan does this only to have the last laugh.

22

The chaos following Radwan's duets with his brother caused a small coup that split their voices up, and soon they seldom sang together. When one of them sang a line the other admired, he joined and repeated it once or twice. Sometimes, the workers loved the song and sang along with it, and the others followed, creating one united singing voice. Muhammad El-Halaby and Radwan split their singing, so that the latter sang for the baker and the front-room workers, and the former for the stove workers and the back-room lifters. Sometimes, as they sang different songs, they raised their voices, as though duelling. 'Lovely Radwan, lovely,' the baker would say, cheering him on so he wouldn't be the first one silenced. Nawwaf, the dough-maker, told Muhammad El-Halaby to forget the bakery altogether and sing whatever he liked.

In the afternoons, after all the workers had left the bakery, they sat together and ate Muhammad's boiled potatoes and eggs out of the same pot, or they sliced large pieces of mortadella straight from the tin.

Radwan ate silently, and peeled, then passed his brother potatoes and eggs, or he sincerely invited Khalil to come and eat with them. In this way, he avoided the boredom that set in when his brother climbed the scaffolds and went to sleep on the flour bags upstairs.

Muhammad El-Halaby used to say that everyone from Halab

had a beautiful voice, but his brother's arrival extinguished his aspirations to become a singer. He stopped talking about beautiful voices, believing that any mention of this would make the workers around him think of his brother, and of the fact that a single bakery can't produce two famous vocalists. This also made him think that maybe if there were two great voices in our bakery alone, it meant there were a lot of good singers out there, and that not every great singer got to be a famous vocalist. And so he began going to sleep right after lunch, and stopped joining me in the front room, in case I insisted that he talk about voices and singing.

Radwan lessened the seriousness of singing by using it to pass the time. But the workers around him didn't seem to mind this and enjoyed hearing him sing. Sometimes he started a verse but didn't finish it, tricking and teasing them with it. 'Damn you, Radwan,' they'd say, not knowing whether to laugh or shout. They liked to watch him sing; it wasn't enough just to hear him. Even the stove workers, who were separated from the back room by the high boards, moved a couple of steps back in order to see him.

When Muhammad El-Halaby and Radwan fought, I ran over to them from the front room to split them up. I knew that Muhammad hated Radwan's shenanigans and the confusion he caused with his teasing, stifled verses. Their voices rose suddenly and blew through the small window that separated the two rooms. As I went over to them, I could picture Muhammad hitting Radwan and pushing him, and Radwan stiffening his body in an attempt not to respond to his brother's blows. Afterwards, they'd calm down and Muhammad would realise that he'd been cruel to his brother, who he was supposed to be taking care of. He would go to Radwan later, apologising, and saying, in a voice that still held his anger, 'How long has it been since you washed your clothes? Give them to me, I'll wash them for you.' If their fights lasted longer, and Radwan got sick of stiffening his body and responded to Muhammad's blows, they didn't make up for hours. Their blood coursed quickly through their bodies for a long time.

Muhammad El-Halaby lost his mind once and hit Radwan all over with an empty pot, and then they didn't speak a word to each other for two or three days. They didn't sing and they ate separately. Radwan would joke around with Khalil in hushed tones. Muhammad didn't make a single sound, even his movements were silent, and no one heard his footsteps fall across the front room. He would eat at the very end of the stove, in the corner, and then stand by the unwrapping machine, smoking a cigarette before going up to sleep. That was his way of apologising; not for the scars he left on his brother's face and shoulders, but for the movements his brother made as he received the blows. He'd release painful sounds as I tried to pry Muhammad off him, those sounds yet another sign of how beautiful his voice really was.

23

Farhat figured out how to split his time between the three or four open windows. It was as though he and Muhammad divided the sleeping and waking women between them, and each now had his private share of windows. But Muhammad still spent his time migrating from one side of the rooftop to another. He had very little time between sunrise and waking time, so he would stop looking at them as they lay in bed and stand in front of another window, anticipating their awakening. Farhat, because he'd spied so intently, knew precisely when the women would turn, or get up, and when their husbands would shut the windows and hide their impending action. In his close knowledge of the timing of their intimate moments, Farhat was like a student who cheated on exams, transferring the correct answers from the cheat sheet to the test paper. Muhammad told Ramez that Farhat knew them from his own house, which was closer to their windows than the roof was. That was the excuse Farhat used to retain the rights to his windows; like he wanted to take on full responsibility when the women caught him and loudly protested at his spying on them in their sleep.

The appearance of the women at their small kitchen windows signalled the end of Farhat's spying. They became immersed in housework, their bodies hardening with their toil, having been softened with sleep.

'To the *za'atar* bread,' Ramez would say. He spent the morning running from one window to the other with no luck. It seemed that as soon as he left one window, the girl would get naked, and by the time he got to the other, she had put her clothes on. He thought he would never get as lucky as Farhat, and hated it. 'The *za'atar* bread is getting cold,' he'd say, taking it out of the bag and lifting it up high so the other two would come over and join him.

Farhat's friends who came over to the roof to rest from all the studying of the day looked as exhausted as if they'd used their hands and bodies to study. Ramez sat quietly and refrained from laughing at the jokes they made. He thought the jokes boring because they came from notebooks and textbooks, and conversations with teachers. In seeing them laughing at a joke, he saw their minds and bodies shrinking in age. With Farhat and Muhammad laughing too, Ramez felt he'd won something by not joining in, and that he'd fallen from their circle. He looked at his watch and said he was late for work. While they continued talking, he made to leave, but it took him forever, and he kept walking over to the roof's door and coming back to them.

To get them to act the way they used to around him, he stole the car from in front of the bakery. He was thinking of taking his brother's white car since his brother had been using the Fiat to go home every night after work. Ramez parked it up the street from the house so that his family wouldn't hear the engine as he drove off. He was afraid they'd wake up and see him in the car.

Farhat and Muhammad were sleeping on the roof. He didn't wake them artfully this time, but just whispered for them to get up. Farhat woke up knowing that since it was night time and Ramez was there it meant he had brought the car. 'Let's go,' Ramez said, 'Hurry!' and he raced ahead of them down the stairs. He had left the door of the bakery locked and the workers sleeping inside. Farhat slipped into the car and sat in the passenger seat, asking what time it was. 'Where's Muhammad?' Ramez asked, and flashed his lights to urge him down the stairs. Farhat told him to put the car in neutral so that his parents wouldn't hear them leaving.

Muhammad walked away from them, and Ramez yelled for him to turn around. He tried to get in the front seat by Farhat, but Ramez threatened to drive off and leave him. Muhammad got in, slammed the door shut, then opened and slammed it again to annoy Ramez, who was trying to be stealthy. He asked Ramez if he was driving them to the bakery so they could study. Muhammad was joking, and right after he said it, he realised that he'd missed this, that it had been ages since he'd joked in the car, because of all the time he was spending living up on the roof.

24

After all the workers went home and Muhammad El-Halaby climbed the steps up to sleep, his brother rushed out to the front room, as if he was calling the customers back for more bread. He headed from the sink to the oven, then suddenly turned to the stove, as though he'd just remembered something, and stood in front of it, staring at the dark space beneath him. Then he went to the dump behind the oven, and stood there, before climbing the stairs to the sleeping area and standing in the middle of it, peering down at the scaffolds to see what they looked like from above.

'Come look,' he told Khalil, who ignored him until he grabbed him by the hand. 'Look at that cockroach,' he said to Khalil, and reached out to grab it by the antennae that darted from side to side. As soon as Khalil realised that Radwan planned to terrify him with it he kicked his foot forward into the corner and slammed it down on the cockroach over and over again. 'Ha! He got away!' Radwan said, and lifted his fingers up to scare Khalil, even though there was no roach in them. He pinched his fingers really tight and brought them close to Khalil's eyelashes, then separated them to show that there was nothing in them.

Khalil steeled himself against Radwan's threats, until a woman came in to buy her bread, or a man went up to use the bathroom. 'Hello, sir,' Radwan said to the shoe-shine, and the man ran up the steps to relieve himself. 'Quick, quick!' Radwan said to him from the first floor, eager to get back to his shenanigans with Khalil. The shoe-shine was a small man who wore really thick glasses. 'How can you see with these?' Radwan asked, trying them on and waving his hands in front of his eyes, which were crossed behind the lenses. He took them off to give them back, but faked dropping them on the floor to watch the man's reaction: a nervous jump like the kind a child would make.

When the Armenian woman who owned the antique store climbed up the stairs to use the bathroom, Radwan sat bent over on the bottom step and pretended he was her. 'Damn you, Radwan,' she said when she saw him blocking the stairs. He took his time to move out of her way so he could stare at her legs as they descended the steps, and so she wrapped her skirt tightly around them, or ran back up the stairs and waited. Still, she smiled when she told him he was naughty and that she was old enough to be his mother. I asked him if he was truly interested in her or whether he was just joking around. He answered that she was not like other women, and he waved his hands around, and clasped them together in the shape of a shell. Then he said that he wanted to make love to her in the corner by the stacks. 'Over there,' he said, and nodded his head in the direction of the corner.

'Over there,' he said again, and pointed, but Khalil didn't look, just kept staring at Radwan's face and hands. Radwan started to act out what he wanted to do to her, pretending to lift her leg up high, and I told him to leave Khalil alone. He said that this was good for Khalil; that he'd stay shy if he didn't learn how to crave women. I told him he did crave them, he just didn't stare at them, and Radwan lifted his hand and rubbed his head with it, as if turning over the words he'd just heard, and trying to understand.

25

With the two sisters Muhammad El-Halaby never tried to say that it was one girl for me and one for him, because they weren't his type. He was waiting for his big break as a singer, and his type tended to be one of those girls who worked as a hostess in clubs, the kind of girl who sat with customers but didn't let them touch her, or looked so pure that people thought she was the club owner's little sister or nanny.

That will tell you something about Muhammad El-Halaby's mysterious place and rank in the world of singing. These women were his type because he did most of his performing at nightclubs. He didn't want them to be too educated, but not illiterate either. Instead he wanted them to have a yearning to write. It wasn't that they had to be equals – he was a terrible writer – but because he wanted them to have an aspiration outside of night-club work. That way he felt they were deserving, as writers with aspirations that matched his own. They wouldn't be good enough for him when he became a famous singer, but they were fine now, for an aspiring vocalist who worked at a bakery.

When Radwan came to work at the bakery, and Muhammad began to sleep upstairs and seemed to shed his ambitions, or at least to put them on hold, I had to come up with a different type of girl for him. I couldn't really imagine what kind of woman he would be with in the future because I didn't know how much he would change. If he quit singing for a long time it would probably be good for him to be with a woman from Halab, his hometown; a woman who knew how to write like the women at the nightclubs, since he was practically illiterate. That would be a good match for him, because even if he kept his voice quiet, like a watch someone tucks away in a cupboard, under a pile of clothes, he'd still have it. It would still be there, in his throat.

There's nothing harder than finding the perfect match for someone. You can't assume that the perfect match for the bookstore clerk is a female bookstore clerk, or that Khalil's ideal girl would have the same kind of brain that he has. Khalil wouldn't be happy with our choice for him, because he might not have thought a girl who walks with a limp, shifting one side of her body heavily before the other, was sexy. Maybe he'd have preferred a mute girl who couldn't hear what people said but had the right mind and physique for him. The bookstore clerk didn't like the girl who worked with him. Instead he spent his time flirting and joking with the female university students who came in, and with whom he acted like he owned the store. The students flirted and joked back, but that was as far as they'd go, because they knew he was self-educated, and that he was a clerk at the store, not the owner.

It's as if no one was perfectly suited for anyone else. Muhammad El-Halaby didn't just leave the girls to me, he left all girls to all men. He never looked at any of the women who came in the store because he never came to know what kind of woman was perfect for him. And the bookstore clerk kept flirting and joking with the female university students, convincing himself every day that he was getting better at doing so. As for Khalil, he was the only person who knew whether or not he understood women. Myself, I looked at the beautiful sisters who knew what to do with their looks, and how to flaunt them, but I understood that I was more like the bakery workers than the university students, so I just kept slowly counting their loaves of bread and slowly walking them from the back room to

the front. When one of them came in after church and picked up her
order I became convinced that I would have to pick the one that was
less beautiful than the other. But I still remained shy around them,
and so I started to imagine that they lived in an ugly house with only
two bedrooms in it; or that their mother came in and discovered
a serious imperfection the girls had overlooked. I pictured her, for
example, walking over to one of them and finding something stuck
in her teeth, then picking it out. Sometimes I imagined their mother
walking around with her large thighs bare, bending over to pick up a
lira that someone had dropped on the floor.

26

The arrival of Abd the Moroccan to the bakery to visit my father always made my uncle turn towards the back room and grimace, making fists and looking like he wanted to squeeze someone or something. This, incidentally, was one of his many signature moves, and it meant that he was about to go crazy, or that my father was driving him mad on purpose, and that, more than likely, he'd like to grab the guy by the waist and squeeze him, the way women wring water out of newly washed clothes. After doing that he'd face the front room, staring at Abd the Moroccan for a long time, imagining himself grabbing the man by the hair, picking him up off the chair, dragging him across the room, and dumping him in the garbage pail.

This was a likely scenario. My uncle was large and strong, and Abd the Moroccan weighed, according to my brother's estimate, between thirty-five and forty kilos. Despite his diminutive frame, he grouched and never smiled at anyone. 'Where does your father find these guys?' my aunt's husband would ask, joining my uncle in his annoyance. But when my aunt's husband walked through the front room he reached out to Abd the Moroccan, shook his hand, and begged him to stay in his seat. Returning, he repeated to my uncle, who was leaning against the delivery van, 'Where does he get these guys?' He didn't just mean Abd the Moroccan, but Mahmoud too, who my father also claims is a relative of ours.

But Mahmoud didn't come to the bakery often. When he did, he just stood in the corner and waited for my father to speak. Once my father began Mahmoud wouldn't stop talking. 'Calm down,' my father would say to him, and these were usually the words he saw him to the door with.

'They really got him this time,' my father would say in my general direction, since I was the only one left in the bakery after Mahmoud's departure. Or he'd say, 'They're really after him, just him.' I didn't ask him what 'they' did to him, because I knew he wouldn't tell me, or he'd say they didn't do anything, letting me know he didn't want to talk to me about it.

As for those who'd 'get him,' they were unknown to my father and to Mahmoud and even to Abd the Moroccan, who sat quietly as he listened to the details of their latest deed. They were against my father and his friend, or they were against Abd the Moroccan and his friend, but the friend was always targeted, to the point where my father felt he could know nothing about them without him.

My father drew lines on the top of the white tobacco tin, then wrote letters in the boxes the lines made. Sometimes he summoned 'them' and started to talk to the letters he'd drawn, but they didn't answer him. He told those standing around him that they hadn't answered him this time, as though implying they'd done so in the past.

Abd the Moroccan could summon them whenever he wanted. He spoke in a dialect that wasn't solely Moroccan, since it was full of spirits, according to my father. Summoning them, they answered him, but no one else heard. He translated their words to my father, telling him that everything that was stolen from Mahmoud's house would be returned to him. 'Are they the same people who stole from him last time?' my father whispered, so that he didn't interrupt the flow between Abd the Moroccan and the spirits. Abd the Moroccan answered that they were, and my father's face was blank, as though he hadn't heard a thing. I asked my father who they were, and he told me that it was only important that we understand their message, and that the soothsaying argument between them and Abd the Moroccan would only remain in the realm of the spirits, never coming to actual blows. My father said that they were not like regular thieves, because they didn't need to enter people's homes to take their things; they just stole them from far away. 'That's what needs to happen,' he explained, 'to return Mahmoud his things: they have to send them back from far away.'

27

With his brother at the bakery, Muhammad El-Halaby spent his afternoons asleep upstairs, until a new front-room worker started to show up every night and drag him out of the bakery. 'I'm going out,' he'd say to me in a sleepy voice, without even looking at me. He thought that my standing between him and his brother when they fought was proof that I was ignorant of what it was that bound them. It was like I, who was nine or ten years his junior, simply seized the chance to stand between two workers in my father's bakery.

If I couldn't stop his body's blows with my two arms, or with my legs when my arms were hooked onto the scaffold, I shouted at him, 'That's enough, Muhammad, leave him alone.' He'd think about what I'd just said, even though he never acknowledged me, but kept looking at his brother, and hitting him on the face and chest. Then he'd turn and shout a series of obscenities to let me know that my presence didn't stop him from venting his anger.

He started going up to the attic to sleep after work, not only to avoid his brother, but to show me that, he too, could ignore what had been between us. I knew he tossed and turned a lot up there on those flour bags, before he fell asleep. As he lay on the bags he remained aware of people coming in and out of the back room, beneath him. Radwan never teased Khalil loudly if Muhammad was asleep, and when he did, Muhammad would peer over the scaffold and stare at Radwan for a long time, saying nothing. Once, Radwan went up the stairs and opened the bathroom door on Khalil, to see if he was masturbating, and Muhammad ran over and attacked him, to let him know that napping didn't keep him from wanting to hit him.

The thing that kept him upstairs day after day was the sound of his brother's laugh, followed by my own. He thought I'd traded him in for his brother, and that I'd begun standing in the doorway to the back room to keep Radwan company. Since we were close in age, Radwan and I, Muhammad believed that we plotted to distance him from our circle. Radwan was very fond of joking around, and loved to raise his head up in the direction of the rafters and laugh loudly, or burst out in song.

Muhammad wouldn't have gone out with the new worker at night if he wasn't bored from all the hours he spent alone during the day.

My father, upon arrival, had the same sleep-swollen face as Muhammad, and he asked me if I'd sold all the bread, heading over to the shelves to see. It was the same thing he did when he asked if the yeast-seller had come by – he walked over to the end of the stove and checked the box where we keep all the yeast. If he pointed his finger in the direction of the flour bags upstairs, it was his way of asking if Muhammad El-Halaby had gone out again tonight. I said that he had. He grimaced the way my uncle did, because he hadn't had enough sleep, and it would be another five or six hours before he could go back to bed. 'Why's the bakery so dirty?' he asked Khalil, who swept the floor with his eyes first before going to get the broom. 'Has Muhammad El-Halaby come back?' Khalil asked, and I told him that he hadn't.

Soon, another Muhammad El-Halaby arrived, our Muhammad's cousin, and the baker loved to call their names and see them both turn to him at the same time. 'No,' he'd say, 'not Muhammad El-Halaby, Muhammad!' They quickly understood that he was taunting them for his own private amusement over there by the oven. Sometimes he'd turn to Radwan, who was sifting the flour, and say, 'Hurry up, Radwan El-Halaby, hurry up!' For a while, my father was able to separate them by calling them by their job name: there was Muhammad the front-room worker and Muhammad the unwrapper. But it was hard to call them that when they were alone. For example, my father couldn't say, 'Come here, Muhammad who works in the front room.' In addition, he had to write their full, real names in the large register, in the section for employees' wages, and he couldn't very well use nicknames there.

'What is your family's name of origin?' he asked the Muhammad El-Halaby who worked in the front room, and that one answered, 'Sir, its name is El-Halaby, and that's what they call me in Halab.' It was clear, right from the beginning of his employment here, that he would be the one to keep his name, because he seemed to take himself seriously and treat it with respect, as though he was a learned clerk. Showing up to his shift early in the evening, he'd sit with my father and talk to him as though he'd just come in from his huge house on the hill. This bothered the original Muhammad El-Halaby, and when he came down from his nap and saw them talking this way he felt like a bakery worker among learned clerks, and that he was being completely ignored.

In the register we wrote his name down as Muhammad Rajiha, the name that was on his ticket from Halab. My brother and I began to refer to him with that name, too, whenever we talked about the workers. He didn't hide the fact that he hated this name, and that the feminine 'a' at the end of it made him feel like a girl. The baker sensed his embarrassment and began calling him by his last name. 'Sing us a little something, Rajiha,' he'd say, laughing, remembering the names of belly dancers, singers, and other women's names the workers loved to make fun of each other with.

28

Ramez beat Farhat to Egypt. He couldn't wait for him, even though it would've been more fun if he had. Farhat would've also been a great help in filling out paperwork at the airport and the hotel, because these are things students know how to do, even if they never actually learned them at school. But Ramez hurried off anyway. He said he didn't want to wait another three months, possibly four, for Farhat to fail the first round of exams, then the second. Farhat's parents wouldn't let him go until the end of summer vacation, at which time the names of everyone who passed the exam would be posted and Farhat's name wouldn't be on it. He tried to convince them by saying that since he'd fail anyway what difference did it make if he stayed? The only studying he did, his father said, was for the test to be a failure, and that a failure here would be a failure in Egypt.

Back on the roof, Farhat couldn't convince Ramez to wait. He spoke slowly and calmly with movements that tried to portray how if they made the trip together it too would be slow and calm, and sensible. Muhammad imitated his movements mockingly, and Farhat gave him a look, but said nothing. Ramez was enjoying Muhammad's gestures, and asked him to show us how the sellers take pairs of underwear out of their boxes. Muhammad started making obscene gestures at Ramez and Farhat quit his speech in despair.

Ramez and I stood outside the airport waiting for his flight. He was wearing a polka-dot suit, which he must have kept on the entire trip, because he didn't take a suitcase and was wearing it in the only photo he brought back. Taking his ticket out of his pocket, he reminded me not to tell anyone that I'd seen him leave. He asked me what I wanted him to bring me back from Egypt. He was nervous, not only since he was travelling alone, but because he knew this trip would be hard to hide from his brother. It wouldn't help that he was only going for a short while (a *really* short while): two days and a single night. His getting on a plane and sleeping at the hotel would create traces his brother would uncover sooner or later; if not that week, then a year from now. 'We came to the airport too early,' he said, shaking his watch and bringing it close to his ear to make sure it hadn't stopped.

In the photo his necktie was too short and barely went halfway down his belly. I'd told him to retie it at the airport, because I saw that it was on wrong, and he said he'd do it on the plane. He was so nervous his hands could barely manage taking out his tickets and the folded Egyptian pounds sitting by the liras in his pocket. He kept checking their thickness every few minutes, running his fingers against the edges and quickly recounting them. He asked again what I wanted him to bring me from Egypt and I gave him the same answer I'd been giving him for two days. Then he said that he would take me with him next time, and that this trip was only an exploratory one, thereby making sure he didn't look pathetic if he came back without exciting stories. But he was smiling in the photograph as he stood by the dark, heavy singer in Egyptian clothing. 'What colour do you want it in?' he asked, meaning the snake-leather belt I'd asked him for. As we stood there in front of the airport, I couldn't tell him what colour I wanted, because he suddenly seemed like someone else, someone brave, who could do things I couldn't.

In the photograph, which was printed on thick paper, you could barely see the men standing behind him, their heads raised, as though his height eclipsed them in front of the camera at the door of the club. He asked the singer if he could take a picture with him, squeezing past all the people in the audience to do so.

'What did you say, exactly?' Muhammad asked when he saw the photograph. 'How did you do it?'

Ramez replied, 'I said: "Sir, singer, Muhammad Taha?" Then, I forget exactly what came after.' He forgot because he was too busy trying to reach the singer and quickly take him to the photographer before someone else did.

'I'll bring you a brown one,' he said about the belt, 'because a black one would look like ordinary old leather.' He extended his arm, but didn't look at his watch, and embraced me. His face brushed against mine, and he laughed, embarrassed, because he felt he was behaving the way travellers do. I almost laughed too, since I was going to see him the following day, before he even changed his clothes.

Muhammad told him he must have done nothing with the ladies, if he spent his whole evening listening to Muhammad Taha. Farhat, clutching at the photograph, said that you can't do anything with them on the first night anyway. But Ramez said he knew how to get them right away, or even have them come to him. 'Egypt is easy,' he remarked, his words slamming into the three of us. He was going to continue telling us all about this until he saw Muhammad blowing on the photograph and wiping it with his sleeve.

'Give me back the picture,' Ramez said, 'Give it back.' He went over to get it, and whispered into my ear that I shouldn't tell the others about the belt. 'You!' he said to Muhammad, 'Listen and learn.'

Muhammad answered that he should be careful who got his hands on the photograph; his brother might see it and hit him. This didn't annoy Ramez at all, and he told him that he would frame the picture and put it up in the bakery for all of his brothers to see.

29

Abd the Moroccan came to our house for the sole purpose of terrifying my mother. She saw him standing at the door, his face dark and hair inflated like a balloon over his face, and she took a few steps back, slammed the door quickly and hid behind it. 'Why doesn't he ever ring the doorbell?' she asked my father, who teased her, saying that he preferred to rap his knuckles against the door. 'But then he just stands there for fifteen minutes, half an hour, and waits,' my mother said. My father kept teasing her, saying that he liked to stand and wait, because he knew we were inside. When she ran off angrily to her room it wasn't because she was afraid of the magic he might do on us, but because of the Armenian neighbours seeing him come over. She thought my father was destroying his reputation by inviting the man in and sitting with him. In fact, Abd the Moroccan seemed to have brainwashed him, because my father could no longer go to sleep without lighting a few sticks of incense. He also thought it was normal to say things like, 'Abd the Moroccan can get things out of walls. I saw him do it once. There were people crowding around him, and they didn't believe he could do it. They laughed at him when he ran around the fire, chanting magic words to get the spirit out of the wall. After he got it, he turned it in his hands for a while, then passed it down to the others. They each looked at it one by one, and a woman in the next room began to scream, because the spirit was leaving her body. I myself wouldn't have believed it if he hadn't turned it over in his hand, two or three times, before tossing it in the fire.'

'But what was it?' my mother asked. She was still having a hard time getting used to this kind of talk. She again said that he was ruining his social standing by hanging around these strange men who fooled him and took his money.

My aunt's husband said he would believe in Abd the Moroccan and Mahmoud Faqih if they brought him the lottery's winning numbers before Thursday. My father told him that the lottery came out every week and that they needed nine days to figure such things out, and so my aunt's husband knew he was just making things up. 'Well then,' my aunt's husband said, 'why can't they find out what the one after that is? It's not for another fourteen days.'

Except for the incense sticks and the lines on the backs of tobacco tins, no one ever saw any proof of the magic my father liked to talk about. Out of all the things he said, they found nothing they could see or touch. 'We got them to return Mahmoud Faqih's things,' my father shouted happily, as if giving us some long-awaited bit of great news. At the end of the soothsaying session Abd the Moroccan called Faqih and told him to look in the back of his closet for his things, and that they'd be right where he'd left them. Faqih couldn't believe his eyes when he found them, and he came over and told us all about it. My aunt's husband told him they would just steal it again, and my father stared at him for a long time, as if to say, 'Even if they do, we'll find a way to get them back.'

'I mean,' my aunt's husband corrected himself, 'what if they do steal them again? Have you taken any precautions to make sure they won't be able to?'

Had my aunt's husband believed in magic, he would still never accept that my father was capable of practising it. He stood outside the bakery and told people that the whole theft and return thing was a charade. My uncle wasn't too worried about it, because he didn't think it affected the bakery's business, but nonetheless, he shook his head to indicate that he was running out of patience with my father. A few days later his movements became more frantic when my father told him a story about how some people he knew were digging through the earth with shovels in search of treasure. My father told him that they couldn't get it because a djinn hit one of them hard against the face, leaving a long gash from ear to throat.

Here, my uncle's movements became indecipherable, but my aunt's husband knew that they converged and encapsulated everything he wanted to say about my father: 'How can a man this crazy work with customers, and pay for the workers, flour, oil, and yeast-sellers?'

30

We saw Peter the American on our way down to the beach, and he laughed when he saw how many of us were stuffed in the car. He'd never seen the workers all together outside of the bakery. They responded by waving their hands and yelling, 'Peter! Peter!' and then they laughed, because they remembered how shy he looked when he came into the back room and hurriedly climbed up the stairs to the toilet. Upon reaching the high stone steps, Radwan and I raced, with Muhammad El-Halaby following too, to show us that he could loosen up when it was time to relax. I stood half-way up the high stone steps and waited for them because I was their only guide to the shore.

My father told me that my brother would meet us there and that we should all stick together so nobody got lost. So I waited and watched them from the bottom of the ladder, as all of them climbed down, including the baker whose long legs weren't a help to him now. He had agreed to join us, even though it meant that his family would have to spend the first day of Eid alone. The stone-table workers came, too, and asked Muhammad Rajiha to join us, saying that no one spent the first day of Eid alone, in a shut bakery. But he refused, and the whole way over the workers kept asking Radwan, 'Don't you wish your brother would have come along?' They asked him this again as they stood behind me when I was paying the beach-stand owner for us all.

I put the change in my pocket and the baker asked what we would do next. Muhammad El-Halaby told him we would take our clothes off in a cabin and change. Then he asked if he had brought a swimsuit with him, but he hadn't. Khalil had come empty-handed as well, but luckily they were able to rent them from the beach stand. He stared at all the trunks hanging on the rope, trying to find his size. The baker found one right away. It was baggy and had a thin rope to tie around the waist. I turned to pay the beach-stand owner again, and then Khalil emerged from the changing room with short swimming trunks and a small towel folded over his arm. After him came Nawwaf the dough-maker, patting his stomach hairs with his palm self-consciously, and embarrassed about baring his body in public. Just as I was about to shut the cabana door behind me, Hussein's lithe body passed by me quickly.

We were among the first to arrive at the shore. My father told us we'd find everyone else asleep, and as he shut the bakery door he'd looked happy to see us off so early, and to enjoy a few extra hours of sleep. There were large wooden displays, their legs sunken in the sand, and on them hung wet bathing suits which had been washed to keep the salt water from ruining them.

Radwan was already at the water's edge, and was acting like he was about to jump into the deeper part . When he saw me standing by the changing rooms he shouted at me to join him, then shivered exaggeratedly to let me know that the water was cold. I walked back to the cabana to see what was taking the baker and Khalil so long, but found them walking over to the seashore. Khalil was glancing at his own body, and the baker asked me if he looked alright in the swimming trunks. His body was pale, with a tinge of yellow from all the sweating he did in front of the oven. As we approached the water his voice sounded thick and phlegmy. The three of us walked over to the rest, where the table workers were fighting without exerting themselves too much. Radwan cheered them on, and they turned on him as if they wanted to throw him into the water.

Radwan started laughing at the baker's trunks, which reached down to his knees. He then started to laugh at the baker's body as well, making the baker rush towards him swearing and chuckling in his thick voice. Everyone patted their bellies with their palms. 'Eh, eh, eh,' screamed Muhammad El-Halaby, then ran off towards the water. He stretched his arms out and looked like a bird, then jumped into the water, and we all understood that he'd meant to surprise us all with his ability to swim, since he'd kept it a secret. His head emerged after a while underwater, he opened his eyes, and shouted, 'Get in, get in, it's beautiful!'

Above, on the flat shore, they all turned their back on him as if to say they were happy to leave the cold water to him. 'Come in, come in!' he called over to Hussein Sari El-Din, the counter worker, who didn't answer and usually didn't talk much. He moved his small but strong body forward to the edge, and dipped his short legs in the water to get himself used to the cold. Radwan and Nawwaf the dough-maker winked at each other, then grabbed the baker from each side and pushed him towards the edge of the water. Khalil retreated to the thick sea wall out of fear that they'd tease him next. The baker grunted loudly at them as they surrounded him, then began waving his skinny, muscle-free arms, which were nonetheless strong-boned, preparing to strike anyone who stood close to him. He walked off towards the shore and the wooden billboards. As he sat in the shallow water and waved his thin arms like a duck, it appeared as though this was the farthest distance he'd go. 'He's getting the water dirty,' Muhammad El-Halaby said when he saw the baker scooping water up with his hands and washing his hair, shoulders, face, and armpits. He dipped his face in the water and leaned back to gargle, the water coming out of his mouth dirty from mixing with his long, yellow teeth.

He sat in the same place even when two women appeared out of nowhere, as though they'd been hiding between the wooden billboards, and passed by the baker. The men standing on the shore all shouted and called to him in code in an attempt to warn him of the two women. He stretched his skinny arms and sprayed them with water, but it didn't go much farther from where he was sitting. He began to talk to them in baker-talk, saying, 'Dough, boy,' to Muhammad El-Halaby, or 'Work, boy,' to Radwan, as if to remind him to stack the hot loaves on the wooden board. The women stood in the same spot, and continued chatting as though they were in a small, quiet bubble and didn't notice us at all.

We'd all gone in the water when my brother showed up with Ramez, who had a gym bag draped over his shoulder. They didn't call out to us, and were satisfied with watching us from afar, waving and making us out from the other swimmers who were beginning to separate throughout the waters of the small bay. Once they were sure we were all there, my brother signalled that he and Ramez were off to the cabanas to put on their swimming trunks. They reappeared, walking down the wide shore, my brother with his chest puffed out and his arms raised from his armpits ever so slightly. He looked like a real body-building champion.

We got out of the water when we got to the end of the gulf, and Nawwaf the dough-maker approached my brother to shake hands with him, though his hands were wet. He tugged at his palm for a minute, their bodies swaying back and forth, then they split apart. My brother dusted off his body, as though to get it back in order again, and then he glanced at Ramez, whose body showed no signs of physical training.

31

My brother rowed the small boat around swimmers and through the water using only one oar. I swam and pulled at it from the front to help get people out of the way, while Muhammad El-Halaby helped push it forward from the back. The baker didn't join us. He was afraid of the water, and Hussein Sari El-Din stayed on the shore because he was beginning to feel seasick. When we reached the edge of the small bay, Nawwaf told my brother we should stop there, close to the swimmers and the rocks they'd built the deck on. My brother said he wasn't worried about the boat sinking. Nawwaf only knew how to swim in rivers, crossing the small distance between their banks. Radwan told him not to worry, that he was here to save him, and his body shook the boat. Nawwaf the dough-maker leaned over to slap him, tipping the boat slightly, then moved his arm back quickly to hold on to the edge. Ramez told my brother to row the boat over to the area where all the women were swimming. The body-builder that was tattooed on Ramez's thin upper arm looked like a mistake from a past life.

'Are you afraid?' my brother asked Khalil, but he just lifted his head up and stared off at the sky, ignoring the sea. When he turned to him and smiled broadly, my brother couldn't tell if this meant Khalil wasn't afraid or was just waiting for him to repeat the question.

The boat cut straight through the waves and Muhammad El-Halaby, swimming alongside us, said he'd race us. He took off energetically, and we watched his flat body in the water. At first he and my brother raced, even though they hadn't begun at the same exact moment the way most racers do. My brother rowed furiously, the muscles on his arms expanding, and Ramez asked him to slow down and take it easy on Muhammad, in case he got tired and dizzy in the water.

Ramez asked if he was tired, and offered to take over the rowing, but Radwan, who sat at the prow of the boat, turned to him and told him that if he did we'd end up spending the night at sea, or drowning in it. Ramez said nothing, just gave him a dirty look, and decided that if he tried to make fun of him again he'd punch him once we reached the shore.

He went after him, there on the boat, with Radwan standing up and rocking it left and right with his feet. But my brother told him to relax and sat him down, then turned and told Radwan that if he didn't stop it he'd throw him into the sea. I told my brother to stop the boat when I saw that Nawwaf's face had turned yellow, and that he was confused and didn't know which way to face. I asked him if he was dizzy, but he didn't answer, just leaned against the edge of the boat. My brother brought the oars in and told us to help him lie down. There was barely any room for him on the boat's deck, and the boat itself was narrower than his body. I turned to my brother with a confused expression, and he got up and came closer. Radwan laughed when he saw us trying to help Nawwaf, lowering his bulky body to the deck. He rocked the boat when he approached us, and Ramez leaned over and punched him in the chest. My brother got up too, and grabbed his head in his palms, squeezing it as though he were cracking open an egg. 'We'll just throw you in here,' my brother said, grinding his teeth and squeezing even harder. Radwan screamed in pain, his eyes watering. My brother let go and Radwan muttered something no one understood, looking around for a place to hide his pain. 'He's going to vomit!' I said, and Muhammad El-

Halaby, who was swimming, told us to splash some water on his face. Muhammad lifted himself up by his hands to take a look at Nawwaf, then lowered himself back into the water. 'Not here,' my brother said, and lifted him up and brought Nawwaf's head to the edge of the boat. Muhammad had moved to the opposite side of the boat to avoid the vomit, then lifted his body up to signal to us that we should go back to what we were originally doing.

Nawwaf felt much better after he'd emptied the contents of his stomach. It was a mixture of clear liquid and chunky bits that we turned away from as soon as we caught a glimpse.

He washed his mouth and beard off with the salty water and said, 'I'm better now,' and stretched out his large body on the deck. My brother asked if he wanted us to head back, and Nawwaf shrugged his shoulders to show that it was up to us. Ramez said we were almost there, and asked my brother again if he needed a break from rowing. Radwan had cleared the space at the front of the boat and was leaning over the edge as though to hide his face from us. Ramez just continued teasing him, sitting in place with one leg dangling out of the boat and an arm hanging onto the edge of its short rudder. My brother speeded up, and Ramez banged his foot against the wooden side of the boat like a jockey. He told me to come closer so that we'd be the first ones to see the cleavage of the female swimmers. Ramez turned to Khalil and asked him to join us as well, but my brother said we couldn't all sit up front because we'd tip the boat over.

'That's a woman,' Ramez said, pointing. 'Hurry, hurry!' he told my brother, banging his foot even harder against the wood. He looked to see where Muhammad El-Halaby was. 'I'm right here,' Muhammad said from underneath the boat, and arched his head so we could see him. 'It's a man,' I said. 'No it's not,' he replied, 'it's a woman.' 'It's a *man*!' I said, but still he insisted it was a woman.

It was a man. He looked at us, waiting for a greeting or something. 'The girls are over there,' Ramez said, pointing at the bay where they were all swimming, and my brother exhaustedly changed the boat's direction.

We didn't stop where a couple of women had broken off from their group to swim, but kept going until we could hear more female voices shouting to one another. As soon as the boat passed the boundary rope suspended in the water, the lifeguards began whistling and shouting in our direction. They were waving and asking us to leave the bay and go back out to sea. My brother, who'd slowed down, now stopped rowing altogether, and stood up to show off his muscles and get them to stop whistling. I got up, too, but this didn't stop them from whistling, shouting, and shaking their fists at us. The female swimmers hung onto the rope and stared at us, turning their bodies away. Muhammad El-Halaby swam to the front of the boat to let the guards know he was with us, and told us we had to turn around. My brother hesitated because he didn't want them to think he was afraid of them, but he turned the boat around slowly, keeping it in place as he did so that his exit from the bay would be slow. As he started rowing, getting us away from the rope, Nawwaf heaved his body over the edge. 'Not here,' Ramez said, as he gazed at the women, as if wishing them goodbye. 'Not here, Nawwaf, not here,' Ramez repeated, and turned to my brother to ask him to row faster before Nawwaf began vomiting into the water where the beautiful girls were swimming.

32

A dark cloud descended on the bay so that it seemed like dusk even though it was barely afternoon. Ramez and I had taken turns rowing so my brother could rest. At times we rowed side by side and rowed at the same time, our bodies hugging the edge of the boat. Each of us held an oar with both hands. Close to the bay's tip, where there's no rope to separate the bay from the sea, we gave the oars back to him and jumped off the boat and into the water, swimming the rest of the way in. The water reflected the overcast sky, and was dark and looked like a sheet of melted tin. Khalil jumped in as well, crossing the short distance to the top deck. We told Muhammad El-Halaby to stay by him and make sure he didn't drown, and we swam by the boat as it headed in to shore. The swimmers crowded the water and many of them had spread on deck and on the sand where the legs of the wooden billboards were sunk. Ramez and I were splashing close to the boat, afraid that our strength would suddenly leave us, or in case we mistook the deep end to be behind us rather than ahead of us. We saw Muhammad El-Halaby helping Khalil get up on the rock that led to the deck. The waves kept coming and slapping him away from it, and we worried that he might drown, or be torn to shreds by the rock's sharp edges. But we kept swimming towards shore.

Hussein Sari El-Din was waiting for us by the billboards, and when the boat made it to shore he grabbed it with his short arms and secured it in the sand. He said he was bored out of his mind and that the baker had gone for a nap in one of the boats that was pulled up on the shore. When he saw Nawwaf the dough-maker step unsteadily from the boat he asked us if he'd been seasick. The baker was still asleep; he looked like someone napping at home. He wasn't on his back like the people sunning themselves, but on his side, hugging his long legs against his belly, his mouth wide open, drooling. Radwan got out of the boat and went over to him. He didn't wake him, or stare at him or say anything, just sat down next to him and began to pile sand onto his legs and between his thighs. We didn't ask him to help us bring the boat in because it was fun seeing him angry like this.

Muhammad approached us, leading Khalil in front of him as though he was guarding him and making sure he wouldn't get lost. We told Nawwaf to just lie in the sand when we saw that he was hovering around us, trying to help lift the boat. 'Take him away,' we asked Hussein Sari El-Din. The boat was heavy with water. 'We have to turn it over first,' my brother said, so we bent down to grab it from the bottom, which was sunk in the water and sand. The baker woke up, and the sight of the cloud and the heavy sea confused him, and he asked if he'd slept too long. He said he wanted to leave and go to see his kids. We told him that Nawwaf wanted to do the same. Hussein Sari El-Din said he would go with them and that Nawwaf wasn't to be left alone. My brother told me that I should take them all back to the bakery, and that they could split off to their own homes from there. Then he walked off with Ramez towards the seaside restaurant, which had rocky steps, and had windows all around so the diners could see the water below.

33

We watched the girls that came to buy bread, cross the street, or browse in the shops, and seeing them that close up – often as close as two people talking to each other, face to face – made us realise what it was that truly separated us from them. Take, for example, the American woman, the bookstore owner's wife. She was delicate, too much so for us. Her leather shoes that she left on the car seat, the house dress that she wore outside, and her short blonde hair, which despite its length was still round and full, all of these made her a woman apart from us, not for us; all these distanced her from us.

But this didn't hurt much. What did were the two sisters. In the back room, I counted their loaves of bread slowly, and stood near them, but they remained far away. It was a chasm I couldn't cross, or come close to bridging. Standing in front of a pile of bread in the back room, I saw so many things that pained me: a pair of dimples, a long neck tickled by a strand of hair, and worst of all, clean, painted toenails. What made it so hard was being so close and yet not being able to touch. With the two sisters, the distance was much shorter than with the American woman, but it was more painful to cross. Then there was the telephone I held to my ear after a certain woman had used it. Doing this, I knew I was widening the gap between us even further, but it helped remind me that it existed, and that the woman was not, and would never be mine.

I watched the bookstore clerk flirt and talk with the girls in front of his shop, picking up their books and turning their pages. He seemed to have bridged a large part of the distance. So I asked my brother, 'Does he do anything with them? Does he get anywhere by doing this?' My brother winked and shook his head, and said that people like the bookstore clerk have to do even more than that to get anywhere at all. He spoke to them all, but got nowhere with any of them.

Radwan knew how to narrow the divide. When the Armenian woman came in he sweet-talked her, and she laughed and sweet-talked back. 'Where should I take her?' he asked me, already knowing the answer: into the narrow alleyway outside, by the dump. It helped their sweet-talking that they did it when she was fresh out of the washroom, where she was so close to her sex, and where Radwan liked to barge in on the workers as they masturbated. He thought they all did it, thinking of women they'd seen or ones they wanted, facing the narrow wall or the door. That was because he did it when he was in there, ignoring the smells that wafted up from the toilet. His fantasies about women and their sex chased out the smell and dirt from his mind, so that, in the corner, he looked like a frozen, ashen-grey statue.

34

Spiritual science didn't take the place of medical science for my father, it just distracted him from it for a while. Instead of reading his medical book, he spent his time drawing lines and letters, and lighting incense, which he liked to burn while he was sleeping. He still cured illnesses when people came to him with symptoms of things like jaundice, anxiety, arthritic fingers, and bladder infections. If someone came in with a rare disease they couldn't name, my father would blend many potions together and tell his patient to take the mixture out into the moonlight and chant words and prayers over it, things that didn't actually affect or change the concoction in any way. He may have believed that borrowing from spiritual science and adding it to medicine benefitted both. His patients, who had come from hospitals and clinics, humoured him by listening to his advice, but they didn't do what he told them to. He knew that the interested looks on their faces were masks, and that they didn't plan to buy any of the potions he advised. Sometimes he got angry and told them they weren't giving the cures a chance. He'd raise his voice angrily and say, 'Just try it, people. I'm not asking for anything more than that,' and by using the plural, he'd let his single patient know that he was fed up with everyone like him – other patients who ignorantly and stubbornly refused to heed his advice.

Now that he was preoccupied with spiritual science, he began to ask his patients right away if they'd take his advice or not, before actually giving it to them. If they answered that they wanted to hear it first, he'd tell them to go visit their doctors and leave him alone. Sometimes he'd tell them the names of one or two specialists at the university who could help. 'You should go to see Dr Yacoubian, or Dr Khattaar,' he'd say, and when the patient asked him what they specialised in he'd name-drop some more and evade the question so as not to reveal how little he knew about medicine. I could always tell he was trying to cover up when he started to list off the names of the doctors' patients.

If you bumped into the tall, skinny Dr Yacoubian in his khaki clothes outside the bakery, you'd never guess he was a doctor, he'd say. Or that when he waved at Dr Khattaar people thought he was just another customer, when really he was one of the best clinical doctors in the country. Once, he left me alone at the bakery and went off to the hospital, sick, and on his return he described nothing but Dr Yacoubian's movements. He was wearing a white coat, with the top three buttons undone, over his old khaki clothes. After attending lightly to my father, he jumped up onto the corner of the bed where my father lay. He told him to put his clothes back on, in a whisper the nurses wouldn't be able to hear, then opened the curtain and said out loud that he would see him at the bakery soon, and they'd eat *za'atar* bread together.

My father kept his hospital visit a secret. I myself, who'd sat and waited for him at the bakery, thought he'd gone to the barber and was running late. But he loved to talk, and so gave it away. He told my aunt's husband that he'd only gone in for a second opinion about his intestinal problems; he told others that he'd gone to the hospital in pain and left at ease. He claimed that the carbonated drinks the doctor suggested were not medicinal, and were the same as the bitter coffee he'd been using to feel better. But he began to take bicarbonate of soda a lot, and asked whoever was going to the pharmacy to bring him back the Italian one in the yellow box. He'd swallow the white powder that was paler than flour, and wash it down with water, then shiver and look down at his newly-healed belly. Then he'd pass the box around and tell everyone to take a tablespoon of it too.

35

When we showed up with the dough-cutting machine, the baker said that the inventors in Hammoud Towers thought only of the stone-table workers, who, in his estimation, worked a quarter as hard as he did. It was the same colour as the dough-maker and the dough-flattener: a yellowed white, which in turn was the same colour as old, dirty dough. There was nothing in its design to betray the inventors' interest in aesthetics. It was square and angular, with a feeder that resembled a constantly open mouth, and had a blade that was shaped like a fan, which slowly turned to cut the dough into palm-sized pieces that Hussein the cutter would pick up and spread on the cloth liners. With its arrival his job became simpler. He would put the huge chunk of dough into the machine's opening, then pick up the slices (which we used to call cuts before the machine's arrival).

Its advent also changed Hussein's job description: he was a slicer now, not a cutter, though he decided to stay at the oven nonetheless. With the machine on the floor, it was the same height as Hussein. Lifted up onto the stone table, Hussein's arms couldn't reach all the way to its top, even when we gave him a tall stool to stand on. He told the other workers that his job was easier now, and showed them the palms of his hands, which were calloused at the edges from all the cutting he'd done. Laughing, he said that now, on the stool, he was taller than Nawwaf and Muhammad Rajiha, who both worked to his left.

The machine did most of his job, taking the dough and pushing it out in round, heavy stacks. All he had to do was put the huge chunk of dough into the opening (which, admittedly, required a lot of strength), and afterwards, stack the balls on the cloth lining. Because he had so little work to do he took great care in the stacking, so that the balls were geometrically placed no matter which angle you viewed them from. They looked, in fact, like a mosaic. But Muhammad Rajiha enjoyed messing the stacks up when he took six dough balls to flatten with his own machine. He didn't do this to anger Hussein, but because the new machine was faster than anyone could keep up with. It dropped a dough ball with each rotation of its blade, and clicked as it did so, annoying Muhammad Rajiha and forcing him to quickly pick up the new arrivals. Before we got the machine, Muhammad enjoyed slapping the side of his own machine as if to let Hussein know that it was hungry and in need of dough balls to flatten. Anytime Hussein came up short, Muhammad helped him cut the dough and ball it up, flattening it on his machine afterwards.

The stacks of dough were piling up so much that Hussein and Muhammad couldn't see each other unless one of them took a step back. Every time a cloth would fill up with dough balls, Hussein would pull it forward and drop them all onto the flour. This was his way of having fun while stacking, and of forgetting that his only task was to lift the heavy dough every half hour and lower it into the machine's opening.

The machine exhausted Muhammad Rajiha. It also caused an imbalance in the bakery because it was so fast. Now, the work on the stone table was faster than the work in the back room. The boards would fill up with dough and the back-room workers didn't know what to do with them. Under the pressure of all those boards, the baker would take his shirt off and announce to the workers that he was going home. My father would tell him to stay, and he'd take over at the oven for him while the baker stood on the sidewalk, smoking and watching the world go by. After he was done with his deliveries, my uncle would help too. Even my aunt's husband helped, but he could only handle fifteen minutes in front of the oven. He didn't like to sweat. All the while, Hussein stood silently by his machine, as though he felt guilty that his palms were softening, and that he was barely doing anything at all to earn his wage; guilty about the new machine which gave him a break, but exhausted the rest of the bakery.

36

We went to say goodbye to Farhat, Ramez taking the Fiat now with his brother's permission. So that Farhat could see us pull up as he stood there with his family, we drove it right up to the airport's entrance. We ran over to them and saw Farhat talking to his mother while his father blinked at the surroundings. His father greeted us grouchily, but his mother embraced us and asked after our families. She had pressured her husband into allowing Farhat to leave; it helped that forty out of his fellow forty-three students had also failed the exams. She said her son hadn't failed because he was stupid but because his professors were greedy and strict with their grades. Also, she added that she wouldn't let a son of hers fail another year at another degree that no one could pass.

Muhmmad had failed as well. He acted as if it hadn't affected him at all when he went down to Farhat's house to help bring the couch in from the roof. Farhat's mother asked him what she was supposed to do with her son now, and Muhammad had almost answered, looking like someone whose opinion mattered, but her husband gave him a look to shut him up and remind him that he had failed, too, and had no business talking. The old man said nothing the rest of the time, just grimaced and frowned, watching us from the corner of his eye. Ramez took Farhat's papers and looked them over to make sure they were all in order, and the old man's look deepened and he spoke in single syllables. We understood that nothing we did at the airport would please him, and because of this Farhat was dying to get to his gate, and kept tilting his head back every time he heard an announcement over the speakers.

Before he left town, Farhat would sit in the Fiat, which we took for short rides, silently, already beginning to take his leave from us. In an attempt to bring him out of his cocoon Ramez asked him what he planned to do with the girls in Egypt. 'He shall do it with them,' Muhammad, who sat in the back seat by me, answered for him in the standardised Arabic of the clerks. Noticing that this answer had failed to animate Farhat, Muhammad turned to Ramez and jokingly ordered him to take Farhat home. 'I'll take *you* home,' Ramez told Muhammad, checking to see if his joke had upset Farhat.

Farhat's mother humoured me and said that I might go to Egypt next year. This wasn't her way of saying I'd fail, too, just that I'd be lucky and get to travel. 'Book him a room there,' Muhammad said, finally speaking up now that Farhat's dad had slunk off, and Ramez looked at him and asked how someone who'd also failed could have the nerve to say things like that. Farhat's mother asked Muhammad why he didn't go to Egypt too, and Ramez told her he had better things to do. 'Show her your hands,' he told Muhammad, 'and how you'll be selling underwear at the market.'

On the way to the airport Ramez had told Muhammad he'd join him in an underwear-selling venture. 'I'll bring the capital, you bring the hands,' he'd said. Muhammad kept leaning into the front seat to make a comment, then Ramez would make another comment, and so on, until they recounted the whole scene of Muhammad standing in front of the market building, a long table full of different types of underwear before him, as he took them out of their packets and turned them for his customers who had come to shop at the stores both inside and outside the building.

Now we were joking desperately in front of Farhat's mother, but she understood that we were trying to get her son to laugh. He stood silently and said nothing. Ramez almost gave away that he'd been to Egypt himself by telling Farhat that they wouldn't feed him much on the plane. He laughed quickly to cover up the near admission, and told Farhat to put his passport in his pocket because he wouldn't need it, and gave him the names of streets and clubs in Egypt, all the while looking over to make sure Farhat's father wasn't paying attention. He wasn't. Ramez started speaking in an Egyptian dialect and laughing, and Farhat's mother gave him a strange look. 'You talk like you've actually been there,' Muhammad said, bringing Ramez to the brink of exposure.

Farhat's mother didn't notice, she just leaned into her son and listed off a litany of reminders she'd undoubtedly told him before. He just kept nodding his head impatiently. They both looked at his father, his back turned to them, and we knew we had to wander away from them and avert our glances. He gave his mother his travel documents and approached his father, standing in front of him, not knowing what to do. 'He wants to say goodbye to you,' Farhat's mother told her husband, who took his hands off his hips. We turned and looked the other way when we saw their arms reach out to one another. Muhammad began narrating in a whisper what he imagined they were doing. 'He's kissing his hand right now,' he said. 'He's pulling it towards him. His eyes are filling with tears.' Farhat came over to us. It was our turn. I gave him a few pecks on the cheek and moved out of the way so he could hug Ramez. They had made secret plans, and now shook on them, their hands firm.

He headed off into the airport and his mother waved to him, teary-eyed. She almost ran after him to say goodbye again, but her husband yelled and asked her what the hell she was doing. Farhat kept turning and waving at us every few steps, until he was swallowed up by a crowd of travellers. Ramez waved back and made hand signals that meant he would catch up with him soon enough. Farhat continued along on his way to his plane. We saw his head and back whenever the crowd around him parted, but he no longer looked back at us. Not even a final glance before boarding and from where we would disappear from his sight.

37

Bald Abu Qassem kept visiting the bakery but he stopped hanging around the stone table workers. He noticed that Hussein was busy picking up dough balls, which fell from the machine's mouth, and stacking them on the cloth liners. What kept him even busier was the machine that injured Muhummad Rajiha, which quickly popped out the flattened loaves. Hussein would get nervous for him, or would help take out the loaves, which he'd stack and sprinkle with handfuls of flour. This was proof from Hussein himself that there was no need for half his tasks. It was also proof that there was no need for the cloth liners, which stacked up on the stone table.

He spread himself out between his machine's opening, its falling dough balls, the cloths that were stacked one on top of the other, and helping Muhammad Rajiha, the dough-cutter. Hussein was therefore unable to sit down with Abu Qassem and hear all the news about the workers who were now wrestlers.

'What happened?' Hussein asked Abu Qassem, lifting his short arms up to the top of the machine. Abu Qassem sighed because he knew Hussein wasn't listening to what he'd just said. Nawwaf, too, made for a terrible audience, since he'd stopped paying attention to his surroundings after the seasickness incident. (He believed the dizziness was a symptom of something more serious. My father tried to tell him that seasickness only affects the strongest of bodies, but Nawwaf said that he was seasick at home, too, and that something inside him didn't feel right.)

Abu Qassem stopped spending too much time standing around the stone workers. Muhammad Rajiha stopped singing, this brought on by a series of events: his brother's never-ending japes, the changing of his name, and everyone at the bakery annoying him. The final straw was the cutting machine slicing his thumb open, after which he stopped talking altogether. If Hussein asked him a question he'd answer it with a shake or nod of the head, or at the most with a one-word answer, and Hussein would repeat the question in a way that could warrant a longer answer. But he didn't hate the machine that cut his thumb. In the three or four days he spent recovering, for the most part asleep on the flour bags or lazing about the back room, he said it was Hussein's machine, and its speed, that had really hurt him. It made him feel like he needed three hands: one to stack the dough, one to feed the machine, and one to flip the loaves over. 'He's just saying that out of anger,' my father said when he saw Muhammad Rajiha coming down the steps and lifting his bandaged, swollen, thumb-less hand in front of his face. My father stood in the front room and, using his hands and his whole body, in front of an imaginary machine, he explained to whoever would listen how Muhammad Rajiha had to use both hands at the same time throughout the three tasks of his job.

He also spoke to them about how the skin of the thumb can seal off at its base, demonstrating this to them by lifting his hands up high in front of them. Muhammad Rajiha's thumb was separated from his hand, and was unable to heal properly under all the bandages. In the emergency room, the doctor had looked at the bluish, almost black stub and said we'd taken too long to come to the hospital. It wasn't Muhammad Rajiha we'd brought too late, but his thumb. My brother had to go and get it, running to the bakery and back, but it was no good. More than forty-five minutes had passed since it had come off.

The doctor said the thumb was dead, that the blood had ceased to flow through it. The thumb got bluer and bluer at its base, closing up the wound, and was now a stranger to the rest of the hand. Muhammad Rajiha just kept on working at the machine without it, and the workers would lean over and stare at his surviving thumb to see what his other hand used to look like. During his short time among the stone table workers, Abu Qassem stared at the four fingers too, and at the baker and his tongs, and at Hussein Sari El-Din, who stacked the dough neatly then messed it up again, mashing it into one big ball he fed to the cutting machine.

Abu Qassem stared at the workers; he couldn't find an excuse not to join the baker who called him over to keep him company. 'I've made you some tea,' the baker would say; then, 'The tea has gone cold'; then, 'I've put the kettle on again.' Abu Qassem said the baker was making him go deaf with his pleas, and so he left the workers and headed over to the oven. He didn't stay by the oven long, growing bored with the talk of bakers who had left their work to sell empty sacks of flour, or buy their own bakeries, or deliver bread in their own cars. It dulled him to drink tea and stand behind the smiling baker, who loved these stories and stood forever in the same spot. Finally, he found a way to escape. 'How can you stand the heat?' he asked the baker, putting the empty tea cup on a board, and running out of the oven area, fanning his shirt off his body, pretending to rid himself of the heat of the oven's flames.

38

My father told people that the bluish tinge which affected the thumb wasn't what actually killed it, but no one believed him, just as they hadn't believed Muhammad Rajiha's hand would go back to normal when my brother had run back to pick up the thumb. They moved it to the scales and covered it with a piece of cloth that barely touched it, but they never thought it was going back to the hand it had originally been part of, and didn't know what to do with it. It had been moved because they couldn't go back to work after it had fallen there on the floor by the stone table, and they certainly couldn't throw it out like trash in the bin under the stairs. Muhammad El-Halaby the back-room worker turned his machine off angrily, as if to shut it up, and Nawwaf raised his hand as if to strike it, and everyone stared at Radwan, even though he was much younger, and waited for him to tell them what to do.

Radwan didn't actually touch the thumb with his hand, just stood over it with his arms extended, trying to keep his distance from it. When Nawwaf lifted it up, carefully, as though he was holding an animate object, Radwan let out a bunch of screams to keep him away from the table. No one went back to work until they were sure they'd taken enough time off. They helped Hussein stack the loaves slowly, and my father put his head around the door and said they had to keep working, and that accidents were part of life and couldn't be helped.

They stopped working again when my brother showed up to get the thumb. It was wrapped in paper, and my father suggested he wrap it in bread instead, since, according to him, bread was cleaner than paper because it went through a burning hot oven that killed off any bacteria. But he didn't insist on this because he knew a thumb in a loaf of bread would look silly at the hospital. My brother had planned what he would do on his way over from the hospital. 'Where is it?' he yelled, as he searched for it fruitlessly. They told him it was on the table, and he picked up a piece of paper and held it in his hand, waiting for one of the workers to help him.

Nawwaf was the closest to him. He delicately took up the cloth that was covering the thumb, picking it up from the middle, halfway between the nail and the red, bloody end.

They went back to their jobs knowing that the day's work wouldn't be completely done. Hussein and Muhammad El-Halaby split the work of the cutting machine, feeding it and stacking the loaves. They were both afraid of it, and Hussein lowered the dough into it with an open palm, while Muhammad snatched the loaves up quickly. Hussein began to fear his own machine as well, and Nawwaf was terrified of his, because it was stronger than all the others, and he knew it wouldn't just chop his thumb off, but rip his arm out of its socket.

39

Muhammad Rajiha's accident created a nice balance between the back-room workers and the table workers, and their output was finally equal. In spite of that, my father still wanted to hire an extra worker, and he went down to the bakers' café and looked for one who wasn't ruined by gambling and card playing. He told his bakery-owner friends to stay on the lookout for an extra worker. While asking Nawwaf to find him a worker in his neighbourhood, Muhammad Rajiha, standing only a few feet away, overheard him and thought that he was to be replaced.

Muhammad had quickly learned to use the machine, and he didn't even need his thumbs to feed it, but it was difficult for him to train himself to work with his injured hand. He kept it straight as he tried to flatten the dough underneath it, and when he lifted it over the machine it looked like he was trying to keep it from folding up.

Even when he wasn't at work he was confused about how to use his hand without a thumb. He'd turn a match several times in his palms before lighting a cigarette, and juggled his boiled eggs from one hand to another, struggling to peel them. It seemed as if he'd lost several fingers, and not just one thumb. To show me how easy it was to peel an egg, my brother would stand in the front room, hold the egg, and rip its shell off without using his other hand. Then he'd throw the egg in the air a couple of times to show off. I thought that

Muhammad Rajiha could just pretend he still had his thumb and so have the full use of his hand. At the very least he could do ninety per cent of what he used to do before he lost his thumb. The problem was really how it looked: the red spot where the thumb had fallen off resembled a distorted belly button. It looked weird, every time someone tried to shake his hand, because there was nothing to stop the approaching hand's trajectory, so it would keep going, through to the middle of Muhammad's arm. It also looked weird if he put it in his pocket, like a can of tobacco, or a leather wallet.

Zeid the back-room worker was one of the oldest employees of the bakery. 'Welcome, Zeid,' my father always said whenever he saw him standing there among the customers, as if he was one of them. He followed him to the oven, told him how much he'd missed him and that he had almost sent my brother out to look for him. 'Welcome, Professor Zeid,' Nawwaf said, seeing Zeid's winter clothes that made him look like a teacher. Hussein, too, teased him, and asked if he was the extra worker. He didn't say anything, just stood there and waited for the baker to give him his *za'atar* bread. After he had, Hussein and Nawwaf left him alone, because they knew he was a quiet eater. 'Keep them coming,' my father told the baker, 'Keep feeding the man till he gets full.'

Zeid ate four loaves, lost his balance, and rested on the steps. My father said it was too much food on an empty stomach. Then he asked Zeid if he'd walked into town from his village once again. 'That's what he does,' he told the workers that now gathered around them. 'He comes in when he's spent all his money.' He asked Zeid if he knew anyone else that could come to work, someone who wouldn't charge him all the expenses of his trip, forgetting that Zeid wasn't one of the workers just yet.

40

After Zeid started working my uncle began pushing workers out of his way whenever he went into the back room. He'd put his long arm on their shoulders or their waists and ask them to get out of the way and let him pass, even though it wasn't really that crowded in there. This was his way of telling the workers and my father that there were too many employees at the bakery, and that to walk through them was to walk through a human traffic jam. If my father was out of the back room, my uncle turned to me or my brother and sneered, 'An extra worker. Extra, extra,' like the word wasn't a real one, but an invention of my father's. Seeing my father walking through the front room or over to the oven, he'd repeat it loudly, but my father kept walking as though he hadn't heard it. My brother and I knew that it was only a matter of time before my father gave my uncle that look and said, in standard Arabic, 'Why, how eccentric you are.'

Zeid didn't really crowd the back room unless he was helping Muhammad El-Halaby; that's when he bumped the boards into the scaffolds. But no one could sense his presence when he stood at the stone table, helping Muhammad Rajiha. It was my father's belief that an extra worker should basically be there in case of another worker's absence, and to fulfill the tasks he really had invented. He told him to separate the different kinds of bread, or to distribute flour in front of the workers, which they hated, because they preferred to spread it themselves.

In the afternoons, the machines stopped and the oven was turned off and the bakery turned into an 'inn' (my uncle's word) for all the workers. My uncle hated seeing them lounging around, and found jobs for them to do. He asked them to clean up the empty dump outside the bakery, but they didn't move, and looked off into the distance, knowing that a bakery worker was expected only to do his bakery work and nothing more. So my uncle asked Zeid specifically to do this, but my father called to Zeid from the front room, and they stood around doing nothing until my uncle forgot all about Zeid.

They all stayed there, but kept themselves separated between the back room, the sleeping area, and the bathroom. Eating too, they stayed apart, consuming their eggs and potatoes at different ends of the room. Muhammad Rajiha ate by his machine, which resembled a backgammon board, and Radwan ate on top of the empty wooden boards, where he worked. Khalil stuffed his eggs and potatoes into a sandwich, and Zeid carried his on a loaf of bread up to the sleeping area. Muhammad El-Halaby bought vegetables from the Bedouin street peddler and ate them with his meal, as well as olives he kept in a jar by his personal belongings. He spread everything out on a wooden plank and invited everyone to join him. 'Bon appetit, you tidy one,' my father said when he saw his makeshift dining area, praising and making fun of him at the same time.

No one spoke to each other. Ever since Radwan had failed to bring Zeid and Muhammad Rajiha together, he sat idly during break time. He walked around, from the table to the oven to the dump behind the bakery and to the garbage pail, as though looking for something. 'This is from Zeid,' he told Khalil, handing him a raw egg, but Khalil didn't fall for it, just stared at him absentmindedly. Radwan avoided his angry brother, who sat on top of the flour bags in the sleeping area, and when he ran up to catch people masturbating in the bathroom, claimed he had to pee. He'd barge in on someone bent over, their head turned away. Radwan wasn't able to guess in such a short time whether the worker was doing it with himself. Sometimes the worker, his head turned, would slam the door back in his face with both hands, and Radwan would have to stand outside like a loser.

The workers switched the bent nail that functioned as a lock for a real one after Radwan barged in on the Armenian woman. She was pulling herself up, and Radwan saw nothing but her thighs under her flowing skirt, which she had lifted up as she was putting her underwear back on. She didn't wait to find out whether Radwan had barged in on purpose and rushed out of the bathroom as if fleeing a trap, and ran down the stairs. It wasn't until she reached the front room that she shouted, to get her anger out on all the workers; not to let me know someone had barged in on her in the washroom. She didn't turn to me when I approached her to see what was wrong, and kept shouting and cursing until all the workers were gathered in the front room. Fearing they'd attack her, she ran out onto the street, hurling her insults at the bakery from the sidewalk.

Her voice reached us in the back room, where we were hiding from the passers-by who were peering in to see what we'd done. Although her anger didn't dissipate, her curses weakened each time she came to the door to shout new insults at us. The last time she came to the door, she said nothing. She simply stared through the cracked door, thrust her hands on her hips, and turned around, back to her small, narrow store.

41

The Armenian woman began walking four or five blocks to use another bathroom. She had to lock up her store and carry her bag on these walks, so that every time she had to use the bathroom it looked like she was done for the day. Standing on the sidewalk outside her tiny store, she spoke to people coming in and out of the church, and never came back to the bakery except as one of its customers.

My father treated her as such, wrapping her *za'atar* bread in two or three pieces of paper and turning away from her to wipe the stray pieces of thyme that had littered the tiles of the counter. We'd explained to him that she'd cursed and yelled at the entire bakery when Radwan had barged in on her in his need to use the bathroom. My father wasn't stupid; he knew Radwan must have barged in on purpose, and so he lifted his fist up to Radwan, in a mock punch. My uncle said nothing to Radwan, because he spent most of his time on deliveries. But he would tell people, including my aunt's husband, that he would've barged in on her himself if he'd found her remotely attractive.

My brother would pat his belly twice after coming out of the juice bar, just to let her know that he didn't let anything get to him. Then he'd pass by her and walk into the bakery, and she'd watch him silently, not knowing what to say. 'Just to let her know I'm here,' he'd say, getting behind the front counter. If he thought this wasn't enough to tease her, he'd pick up the chair we used to reserve our parking spot in front of the bakery and he'd move it a few metres down to take up some of the space in front of her shop too. This didn't seem to affect her, and she'd turn the other cheek, making him feel like he was teasing the air itself.

He began to bang down the chair loudly in front of her, but this, too, failed to annoy her; she would turn to a passer-by and ask him to take a look at the contents of her store. On his return to the bakery, I'd tell him she hadn't even noticed what he'd done, and he'd go back outside to do something even more embarrassing.

We no longer knew what annoyed her, and didn't know if she was ignoring us or if she really didn't see what we were doing because she'd become a different person and was no longer interested in us at all. 'They'll kick her out tomorrow,' my brother said, meaning the store-owners whose bathrooms she used. I knew that even if they did, she still wouldn't come to use ours. She'd find yet another place to go, one in the building she already used, or in any of the buildings that surrounded it. Or she'd hold it in all day and go once, at the end of the afternoon, in the bathroom of the church at the end of the street.

42

Long distances no longer excited Ramez now that he had his brother's permission to use the car. He'd park it, get out of the car and ask Muhammad if he liked the way he parked. 'You're the parking king,' Muhammad would answer him, but he said the word 'king' in an irritable fashion, to let Ramez know he was sick of constantly soothing his ego. They never went very far, just a single turn around the block where the cinemas were, driving slowly through crowded neighbourhoods, watching the mobs of people. While they'd go into juice or sandwich shops, they'd never enter the ones in the public market. Ramez said the public market's sandwiches were tainted with the bodily fluids that dripped down from the brothel rooms above them. He even stopped going to look at his ladies in the windows. In the first letter from Farhat, which Ramez read to Muhammad, he wrote that the women in Egypt came to your apartment. 'Want something, baby?' they said when you opened the door, then they'd come in and spend the whole night there, leaving in the morning.

Although Farhat described only the way in which the women came to the apartments, never anything more, Ramez imagined that Farhat was the one they spent the night with, naked the whole time, even when they made him coffee in the morning. From there, he daydreamed that he was the one who opened the door for them, and

that two of them came in, one for him, and one for Farhat. He saw
them walking around naked and carrying his cigarette packs. But he
wouldn't approach Farhat's girl because his own would be waiting
for him in his room, and he wouldn't want her to go to Farhat later.
The next day, all four of them would go for a walk on the corniche,
walking arm-in-arm, moving people out of their way. He and Farhat
would have to entertain a different pair, too, just for variety's sake.
They'd keep going until they found a pair they could live with.

Ramez couldn't reconcile his desire to be with one girl forever
with his desire to change girls every day. His fantasies confused him,
not just because they split his desire in half – one wanting love and
the other sex – but because he desired both of these things equally.
He'd love it if one girl came and stayed with him forever, but if she
did, he'd hate having to forsake all the other ones.

Muhammad would stay here, in Beirut. Ramez humoured him
and said he'd take him to Egypt one of these days. 'You go first,'
Muhammad said, knowing that Ramez wouldn't take him anywhere
since he hadn't featured at all in any of his fantasies.

43

'Hello, Peter!' we said to the American bookstore clerk when he came by the bakery. The workers greeted him too, and turned to their work to give him privacy when he went up to use the bathroom. The Armenian woman never said a thing about what my brother did with the chair, but when my uncle parked in front of the bakery she gave him a withering look. She still wore her hair the same way, without brushing the back, and her skirt with the orthopedic shoes that helped her walk and stand for long periods of time. But somehow she seemed different. I thought she spoke to her customers in the many different languages she knew to seem different on purpose. She smiled and said goodbye to them as they left, even if they didn't buy anything, and she ignored us if we stood on the sidewalk. Her flirtatious smile belonged only to the passing customer, and he took it all for himself, making sure that we got none of it. If he kept walking and staring straight ahead, she went back into her small store and tidied up her things, putting them in their proper places, ending one scene and starting another.

My brother stopped slamming down chairs in front of her store; he didn't want to send her an invitation to yet another fight we'd have to have and then make up after. I began to stare off to her side of the street, in sincere hope that her gaze would fall on me, and was prepared to exchange greetings with her, no matter how quiet or hushed. On my way up the street to the bakery I thought of the right word to say to her. 'Bonjour,' the word left my lips hesitantly and almost inaudibly; that way I could take it back if it angered her.

'Hello Peter,' we said to the American bookstore clerk when he came by the bakery, lowering our heads a little to welcome him to use the bathroom as he wanted. He lowered his head too, out of embarrassment, and raced up the stairs as if that would make him invisible to the workers underneath him. Once he came back down he'd slow down at the counter, giving us all a sweeping look which ended on my father's face. 'Poor Peter,' my father said. He didn't mean poor as in penniless, but in the way he says Nawwaf is poor: poor because he submits his strong body to work that deflates and diminishes it. Poor when he tells us he feels sick though he looks so healthy. 'You're strong as a horse,' my father told Nawwaf, calming him down and pitying him at the same time. 'Poor Peter,' meaning his foreignness hadn't got him very far. Certainly not as far as some of the female customers who came in and asked for three loaves of bread, then smiled, and paid for them with crisp, clean bills, which they kept in leather purses. Their bills were nothing like the ones in our cash register, which were piled on top of each other indiscriminately, so that we had to dig through them to find the right denomination.

'Three loaves, please,' the female customer said. She turned to the counter to buy something other than bread, looking for things to sample. My father picked up a small round cookie with his fingers and brought it close to her mouth. 'Please, be my guest,' he said, and she leaned in and took a bite, without her teeth, it seemed, just her lips. Then, she lifted her eyes up to the ceiling to savour the taste in her mouth. Finally, she bent her head in approval: 'I'll take an ounce,' she said to my father, who brought out a white bag smaller than the palm of his hand.

At home, these women ate their bread with the same delicacy with which they brought their crisp bills out of their purses. This helped them measure their lives against the watches they kept around their wrists. They came to the bakery at the same time every day, and drank cups of carrot juice from the juice bar at a fixed time too, before descending the stairs to the street that led them to the gate of the university. They laughed at men's jokes, perfect, light laughs that couldn't be misconstrued for anything more; laughs that were commensurate with their happiness, which they were convinced was insubstantial, but hoped would one day be real.

The bookstore clerk who loved joking with them started to become like them, and my brother never left the juice bar without taking three or four drinks. He wanted his body to be perfect like a wrestler's, and beautiful, the kind of beauty that actually made him more of a distant prospect for the girls. I felt the same way. I didn't know if the white jacket I wore made me look better, or if it impressed them from afar, like the way I leaned against the delivery car as though I was all alone, and there weren't people streaming past.

'Hello, Peter. How are you?' my father said as his guest made his way to the bathroom. And when he was finished, my father would say again, 'How are you, Peter? Fine?' My father thought that they could get along, that this American was like everyone else, but Peter was too shy to talk. Like my father, I began to say hello to the Armenian woman, quickly, on my way into the bakery. 'Bonjour,' I said in barely a whisper. Hearing me, she said, 'Bonjour,' but it was just a word to bring her closer to the way she once was.

44

Dear Ramez,

A sincere, humble, and fragrant greeting to your redolent, pure, kind heart.

So ... I've been waiting for you to write back to the letter I sent you two months ago, but alas ... You said you were coming to Cairo on New Year's, but you never came, and I waited until New Year's Eve to hear something from you. Then I went to a party but I was sad that you wouldn't be there to share in the celebrations with me.

Anyway, it was a really great party. We danced and sang until the sun came up, and it was in an apartment on the Nile ... I met the woman who owns it, she's older than me (over thirty). She shook my hand and I introduced her to my Egyptian friend, the guy I told you about in the last letter which I'm not sure now that you got.

All night she'd leave her guests and come to say hi to me and my friend and talk to me. At first, I was shy, and she said, 'Don't you know how to talk?!' When I answered her in an Egyptian dialect she told me to speak Lebanese because she loves Lebanon and the people of Lebanon ...

After a couple of beers I couldn't stop talking, and then we danced and she encouraged me with 'Oh, wow, you're great,' and your friend was in top form. Halfway through the night I started dancing with another woman and the first one came up to me and told me she was jealous ... jealous over me. I kept dancing with other girls though, and my Egyptian friend told me to be careful not to lose her.

She's older than me, like I said, over thirty ... and in the morning, when the party was over, she asked me to stay over with her. I said I couldn't leave my friend all alone, so that she wouldn't think I was easy ... you know they all think Lebanese men are naughty because we start going with girls at an early age.

I'll introduce you to her when you come to Cairo ... but don't come for just a day the way you did when you came and took a photo with Muhammad Taha, come and spend the night. You can stay with us. We have a room overlooking the Nile, and I'll show you around Cairo.

OK, I'll let you go now ... I hope you get this letter. I hope you're well. Write back, I want to know how you've been.

PS how are the boys in Beirut? Is Muhammad still studying or does he plan on working the underwear counter at the market?

PPS don't worry about my studies, I've figured out a way to pass. My love to all.

Your devoted friend,

Farhat

Cairo, 14/1/1966

45

My uncle bought his own car, so our vehicles took up three spots outside, reaching up to the bookstore and down to the Armenian woman's place. His was at the front, a new, huge Opel the size of American cars. Behind it, there was an empty space for customers and, last, we parked the delivery van, and if it was off delivering things, we put the chair and the empty garbage bin there to reserve the spot.

It was an Opel Capitain, not a tiny Opel Cadet (my aunt's husband bought one of those, and two days later so did Ramez's brother). 'Cars ... ' my uncle said, then described the make and model of his own. 'What, our car's not a car?' my aunt's husband said, parking in the customers' spot and walking into the bakery, and my uncle laughed, nodding his head in the direction of the street, daring him to a race. My uncle said he had work to do, not because he was in a hurry, but because he knew my aunt's husband's car needed a few minutes to warm up before it was fit for the road.

The car was covered up with chador-like fabric to protect it from sunlight and dust, and from the flour that flew off the backs of delivery trucks on their weekly stops at the bakery. 'It's a greyish-white,' he told passers-by who wanted to know what colour it was. If they had a difficult time picturing a white that was also grey, or how the two colours would look blended together, he and my uncle lifted the bottom of the chador a little, just a hand's breadth. Then my uncle would stare at the man's face up close. He lifted up the chador in the front if people asked whether it looked different from last year's model. Sometimes he lifted the fabric all the way to the roof to show them the odometer, the radio, and all the buttons floating in the dashboard.

We didn't see the whole car until the end of the day, when he lifted off the fabric, folded it, put it in the trunk, then sped off. My father turned away from the front window and told us that our poor uncle was gone. He wanted us to think that Uncle was a bit of an idiot, and that the car made him less of one. My brother thought my father wanted us to believe this so we wouldn't start thinking about cars. My father pointed this out again when my uncle stopped in front of the bakery and leaned on his horn. 'Here come the youngsters,' he said, 'here they come.' Outside, my uncle, my aunt's husband, and Ramez's brother all parked back to back, as though merging into one.

What my brother and I knew was that Father would want to sit us down and talk to us, man to man. He'd advise us, telling us all about the expense of owning a car, their problems, their accidents, using these as an excuse for not buying one. He just didn't want to look like he was copying everyone else. He said we should wait a while until the others tested out the Opels, to make sure they were good cars. My brother told him we could buy another kind of car, a Renault, for example, or a Vauxhall, or a Fiat 1500. 'The Fiat 1500 is so small,' my father said, because it was the only name he recognised. My brother told him we could buy an American car, and my father's voice went high and he shouted, 'No, a Rolls Royce, why don't we buy a Rolls Royce?'

We weren't impressed that he knew the name of a car he'd never actually seen. Earlier, he'd called my uncle's car, as it hid under the chador, a Rolls Royce, and he'd asked my aunt's husband as he stepped out of the Cadet how his Rolls Royce was. 'It's over 50,000 liras,' he'd say whenever anyone brought up the subject of cars.

'What's in it that makes it so expensive?'

'What's *not* in it?' my father would say, then boast that its metal was as thick as the metal they make tanks out of. He said that when a car crashed into it, nothing happened to the Rolls, and that its engine was perfect, and its manufacturers sold one per country per year.

The Rolls Royce, his friend Sadeq the Iraqi told him, was the kind of car that sticks out in a crowd. It was one of the old, fancy Rolls Royces, not a modern, normal version. The English company stopped making it twenty or thirty years ago. It was in the garage in Iraq, waiting, covered in a layer of dust like the layer that covered the fabric over my uncle's car. Underneath the dust it was silver: not the colour silver, but *actual* silver, and it's 'this thick' (here my father showed us with his thumb and forefinger how thick it was). 'It's not silver-plated the way spoons and dishes and wedding boxes are,' he said, 'because King Ghazi would never accept something so counterfeit.' He asked Sadeq – who was either a student or a professor, because he spent all his time at the university – how they got the car. 'My father bought it,' Sadeq told him. Sadeq was at least ten years younger than my father, but they were still friends. When he came to visit, he told us his father bought it after the coup, for appearances, not transportation. 'It's all silver,' my father said, and the colour wouldn't be affected if they scratched the surface or hammered a nail into it or keyed it.'

'They painted it at a house-painter's, not a car-painter's,' my aunt's husband joked, but he never said it in front of my father.

'Welcome, brother Sadeq,' my father greeted his friend, seeing him enter the bakery dressed to the nines, looking nothing like a fancy Iraqi but speaking the same way Iraqis speak. Sometimes he came in when my father wasn't there, and my brother accosted him and asked him about the car's horsepower, its engine, and its valves. Sadeq told him it was strong and that its storage cost him an obscene amount of money every month. He said this while scooping up dozens of tiny cookies from the front counter and swallowing them as though to test their softness. My brother was convinced he was a thief because he'd already asked to borrow money from the cash register, claiming that he forgot his wallet back at the hotel. Our father knew this, but he kept greeting him with a 'Welcome, brother Sadeq.' He was convinced that the car was parked in that garage, all the way over in Iraq. Although he'd never seen a car like it, it was there in his imagination, gleaming under all that dust, and enormous-looking when parked between two small cars, not over there in Iraq, but right here in Beirut.

46

Ramez became too preoccupied to go to Cairo, and mostly it was with fantasies about Farhat. He pictured him in his silk, polka-dot robe raising his hand and bringing it down on the woman who was over thirty. She'd say, looking up at him from the marble floor, 'Why did you do that? I've done nothing wrong, my darling.' Or he'd picture Farhat, in the same robe, sitting in a rocking chair and smoking a pipe, staring off at the Nile, or rushing off to pack his suitcase while the woman cried and begged him not to go. In Ramez's mind, Farhat would push her so that she almost fell between the bed and the closet. He blended his fantasies together, and suddenly she'd be on the marble floor again, her dark legs bare and her black hair covering her left breast.

He became too preoccupied to visit Cairo. He didn't want to stay in a bedroom alone while Farhat got to stay with his girl in the next room. Ramez imagined them sitting either side of him in the morning and feeding him breakfast, the woman saying teasingly, 'Don't be shy, sweetheart, eat something.' He imagined that they'd brought him to Cairo to feed him, and that he wouldn't have gone if he'd known he was going to spend all his time sitting silently like that. Then they'd show him around town in her Fiat, but in fact ignoring him in the back seat while they talked and kissed, and held hands. They'd take him to an amusement park or a zoo. It didn't help to picture Farhat in that polka-dot silk robe slapping the woman, because even then they seemed so far away from him. After such a fight they'd spend hours in the bedroom, and Ramez would have to find a way to ignore their moans and grunts. He'd leave the living room and the apartment and go for a walk alone all over the streets of Cairo.

He became too preoccupied to visit Cairo. After his shift at the bakery, he'd go to visit Muhammad who stood behind an underwear counter organising his merchandise. They'd take the counter to the market, Muhammad bringing his time and Ramez the 500 liras.

They couldn't find a place to put the counter, because the sidewalk was full of merchants who'd got there earlier. There was a whole row of underwear sellers on the sidewalk. Muhammad found a spot between them, halfway through the market. He'd shout over to the other sellers, and they shouted back, sometimes leaving their counters to engage more fully in conversation. Then he busied himself with the display of underwear, making sure they were at the right angle to meet customers' eyes as they walked down the street. If Ramez came by, he'd do nothing of consequence. He'd push a few pairs around, or organise them according to colour. Most of the time, he just leaned his back against the building's wall and stared. When a customer showed interest, Ramez got out of the way and paced back and forth, as though overseeing the sale or simply waiting for it to be over. He didn't approach or talk to Muhammad until the customer went away. In any case, they rarely exchanged more than a few words before Ramez got back to his post with his back against the wall, once in a while stealing glances at the counter.

His brother had kept the 10,000 liras. Everyone told Ramez he made him work at the bakery for it so he could make interest from it at the bank. His brother asked him every four to six weeks what he planned to do with all the money. 'Would you like to invest it and become a partner at the bakery in Witwat?' he'd ask, and Ramez would ask why he always offered the bakery in Witwat. His brother would give him a dirty look for mistrusting him. Then he'd turn and walk into the back room and tell Ramez to let him know when he found a better bakery.

Ramez took too long and lost some of his money. When his other brothers asked him, 'Why Witwat and not Qantari?' he asked his brother the same thing, but his brother just said, 'Take the money, just take it.' His other brothers told him to get the money and keep it. That way, they could fight over it again, one by one. They'd all show up and ask for it, telling him he could pick which one of them he wanted to give it to.

They'd played him like a fool. He felt as though he was spread thin and that everyone was saying something different. So he went in on a counter with Muhammad and each day, after working at the bakery, he'd go to the market and stand by the counter until late at night when all the counter boys folded up their wares and put them away until morning. Meanwhile, the 10,000 liras was losing its worth every day. After his brother said he could no longer buy him half the Witwat bakery's share, just a third of it, Ramez shook his head and acted like he no longer cared about anything at all. Then it was that he had to come up with an additional 1,000 liras to buy a third of the share. Soon, he could only buy a quarter of it, then a fifth, then an eighth, until finally Ramez agreed to a share in his brother's bakery whose amount and worth was unnamable and unknown.

47

Even before buying the bread machine, the one that took dough in on one side and brought it out as bread on the other, there were very few bakers in Beirut. Bakery owners couldn't find any, playing cards or gambling with workers at cafés. The workers never came into the bakery to say that a baker had arrived in the neighbourhood. Whenever a baker left a bakery in Ras Beirut he left workers and counter boys in his wake, and they played with the tongs and messed around and, on top of all that, got tired every forty-five minutes. Their average bodies weren't capable of hard baker work, and the dough-workers, who had muscular strength, weren't strong-boned enough to do the baker's job. Standing in front of the oven, they looked as though they were modelling, not working. If the dough-worker walked to the oven to relieve someone, they looked like they were walking down a catwalk, showing their bodies off in front of the bakery owners, who watched them from behind their counters. The workers held the tongs and boards delicately, instead of banging them down roughly, the way a real baker would.

The tall, strong baker with the yellow teeth was the last one we ever had. My father knew we'd never find anyone like him again, anyone who'd be willing to work six months straight without a break. 'He's from the old order of bakers,' my father said, seeing how the workers' bodies weakened generation after generation, and how there would come a time when bakery owners wouldn't be able to find a counter boy to stack loaves on the shelves. 'Stay just one more week,' my father pleaded with the baker, who didn't smile or say anything. 'But I have to go,' the baker said, spreading his arms in front of him to show how swollen and dead they were from the flames. My father begged him again for another week, and the baker asked how much we planned to bake tomorrow.

In the days before he left he worked with his palms flat, making sure he didn't injure them. He'd lift them whenever they hurt, and lowered them to alleviate the heat. Sometimes he'd walk out to the counter and show my father how puffy they were on both sides. They felt thick and heavy to all the workers who grasped them in farewell. Nawwaf told him to buy some ointment for them from the pharmacy, then he jumped forward and kissed his cheeks three or four times. 'Don't make him cry,' Radwan said, who hadn't bid him goodbye yet. Hussein stood on the tips of his toes to reach the baker's cheeks, but said nothing. Zeid, who was always daydreaming, said goodbye last, after everyone had joked that the baker was going on a long trip and never coming back to the bakery. By the time Radwan came forward, the baker was sick of goodbyes, so he patted the back of his neck gently, shook him slowly, and said he was leaving. He passed by my father, who kissed him and told him to take care of himself.

48

My father brought in three or four bakers after that, but they were all crooks and gamblers. None of them worked longer than two days. They'd take their wages from my father, say, 'See you tomorrow,' and never come back. 'You work the oven tonight,' he told Muhammad El-Halaby, and asked Zeid, the extra worker, to help him. Or he asked Nawwaf to help in-between shifts. Sometimes Hussein baked and Zeid did his job on the cutting machine, with the dough-maker before him and the flattener after him. Other times, when there were few customers at the counter, my father went down to the oven and worked for fifteen minutes, then left for fifteen minutes to wipe the sweat away with the white rags we put the *za'atar* bread on.

Radwan stood at the shelves and stacked loaves two by two, and amused himself with this game of musical chairs the workers did. He stared and made fun of each of them, recounting their physical details, until he had to quickly and loudly yell to the person who would take his place. Staring at the steaming hot loaves, once in a while, he found a burned one. He would pick it up, lift it above his head, and sing to it loudly. Then he exaggerated this game and added dance moves, until the person working at the oven reached over and knocked him on the head. Radwan knew that at such moments my father fantasised about him being knocked to the floor, the fist going through his neck and slamming noisily down on the boards. My father told him he'd teach him to behave, meaning that Radwan's brother Muhammad Rajiha was incapable of teaching him any manners. If Muhammad yelled at Radwan he worked faster and harder so that he looked like he was making dough and rolling it out at the same time.

My father stood at the counter, wiping it with a sponge and cursing the man in Borj Hammoud who still hadn't delivered the automatic oven. 'Call him,' he told my brother or me, and we'd slowly lift the handle and dial the number he gave us. We knew that he liked to threaten and curse the man in his absence but would never actually do it on the phone. Then we'd hang up the phone, pick it up again, slowly dialling the number, knowing that the more we called, the closer the man on the other end was coming to actually answering. If my father exhaled loudly, blowing all the air out of his mouth, we knew he'd calmed down, and ask him if he really wanted us to call the guy in Borj Hammoud. 'No, forget about it,' he'd say, stepping out onto the street to get some fresh air.

49

Every other bakery in town got an automatic oven from the man in Borj Hammoud except ours. He made one oven per month, and had to design each one individually, measuring it out for each bakery, like a tailor.

In Mustafa's bakery, they had to move the scaffolds and the contents of one of the rooms up to the sleeping area to fit the oven in because the area was too small; and at a bakery at the edge of Hamra, they had to go in to install it twice because the bakery used to be a house. The man's assistant came and measured the space at our bakery. He said we had to take out the old oven and start building the new one all the way out in the dump, and that it would still extend to the stone table where Muhammad Rajiha, Hussein, and Nawwaf stood.

In the bakeries the installers went to before coming to ours, they liked to shut the doors between the front and back rooms to block out the noise. The inventor would add new scaffolds and gears to the old bakeries, so the scaffolds wouldn't have bread piled up to the ceiling. He also added a small area by the oven, with a mechanism that automatically took dough from the scaffold and threw it into the oven's mouth, spitting it out as bread at the other end. In place of the bakers, who no longer worked in Beirut, bakeries hired boys who did nothing but gather the bread and whose wages never went over four liras.

We waited a week after the new stones and many metal knobs arrived before demolishing the oven and removing its old scaffolds. My father told Hussein that he could do the demolishing while he waited for the new metal oven to be installed. Soon he'd need to find another bakery that hadn't yet updated to the automatic ovens and that needed his services.

We no longer needed anyone to pick up the dough, because the scaffolds pulled it and automatically transferred it to the new section by the cutting machine. Hussein refused to do any demolishing, and said he needed to find another job before all the other workers in town snatched them up. As for Muhammad Rajiha, he never spoke to anyone, and no one ever asked him to do the demolishing, because even when he was working with his cutting machine, all he did was sulk and ignore everyone around him.

The only surviving member of the stone-table trio was Nawwaf the dough-maker, who kept his job since the new oven couldn't make its own dough. My father asked him to keep his eye on the four construction workers who came to take the old oven apart. He enjoyed this job, and came in every morning like an office employee, dressed in clothes he didn't need to change at the end of the day. He looked forward to the new oven being completed and to the fact that he'd soon be the sole supervisor of the two men we'd hire to pick up the bread.

One of those men was Radwan, whose head my father advised him not to keep shaving if he wanted to stay with us. He wrung his neck jokingly, after he'd gently slapped it, and told him he also had to stop staring at the female customers who came to the counter.

Khalil stayed too, but only during the construction. He gathered and transferred the rubble to the pile at the end of the back room. My father explained that he hadn't hired him because he thought the noise of the new oven would go straight to his head and bother him too much, and he claimed that Khalil didn't have the right body for climbing up and down the steps and spraying the dough with flour. My aunt's husband suggested he let Khalil gather the bread and Radwan do the climbing, and my father said that Khalil was incapable of sending orders from his brain to his hand fast enough to gather all the bread without dropping it. He said that he'd look at the loaves, then send a message to his hand to pick them up, and his hand would, and next he'd have to send the message to his hand to carry it, and so on. My aunt's husband shook his head and flicked his hand, and said, 'Understood, understood.'

50

Once the workers were done putting the oven together my father told the inventor that the oven looked nothing like the photograph he'd given us and which we'd hung up on the wall by the counter. Its stones weren't light pink the way they were in the photo and the scaffold wasn't sky blue. The oven itself was completely silver on the inside. Standing by it in the back room, we were unable to see the whole, the way we could in the photo. To see it all, we had to walk around it and look at it piece by piece, as though each part of it was separate from the others, or we needed to climb up to the sleeping area and look at it from above. It was hard to see without the oven-room, which once stood below the scaffold and the ceiling and extended to the place where the old dough machine had been.

It was different from the way my father had imagined it. The metal that reached from the front of the oven to the back looked too heavy; it looked like it would split the ground beneath it in half. The empty space on either side of the oven seemed unnecessary, a substitute for the old dump we used to have behind the bakery. 'It's like we built a room inside a room,' my father said to the inventor, who knew what to say to comfort him since he'd installed dozens of them: he told him he'd soon get used to it. He said this quite happily since he'd made lots of money from the ovens.

Turning it on, the gears and parts clunked and moved slowly, as if it needed workers to push it and make it go faster. The inventor smiled every time my father had a look of despair or anger on his face. 'You'll get used to it soon, soon,' the man said, and told him about another bakery owner who once was angry like my father, but now loved his oven. My father took out the photo of the oven and showed it to the man, who laughed, saying, 'This photo of the oven is for show, not for function. Do you want strength or beauty?'

After the man left, my father knew the answer to the question. 'Look,' he told my aunt's husband, showing him the pointed edges of the scaffolds. The inventor hadn't filed them down and had instead left them sharp as knives, and the metal itself looked like a blend of rust and black. On the places where the metal connected, there remained small dots of tin like pimples all crowded in one spot. 'It's an oven,' my aunt's husband said, 'not a thing for window shopping or a car for cruising around town.'

51

My brother decided to give up training after he got back from his first body-building competition. He was disgusted with the body odour of the other competitors who crowded into the room by the movie theatre stage. He didn't like the way they cursed at each other, or the way they took their trousers off in front of each other. On stage, he hated the way the audience shouted. They were mostly men, and their applause sounded like jeers. At the end of the night, when the time came to distribute the trophies and medals, the judges couldn't decide between the competitors, so several people stood on the wooden step for second place, my brother included, grabbing the others and balancing his body by reaching his foot down to the floor.

He angrily gave up training, even though the heavy American weights would tear his muscles and make his body bigger. But in the months that followed this decision, his body looked better than it had before. The loose (he anticipated some weight gain) tailored shirts he wore suited him, and he knew he looked good. He would turn slowly and look at the person who was talking to him, keeping his chest and the buttons on it straight the whole time. Taking a step back when a customer walked in, he tightened the muscles in his forearms and shoulders. In the new car we bought, which was blue on the bottom and grey on top, he'd reach his arm out in front of my father to protect him whenever he made any sudden stops. He wanted to show my father, who wore a suit but no tie, and grasped the handle above his head, that he was strong. My father liked sitting next to his strapping son in the new car, and having his other one sit silently in the back, like a man.

He liked to think of us as his sons, but also that all three of us were men, riding around in a car, going to do some task that only three men could accomplish – even if we were just going to visit my aunt. He liked it when we walked into people's houses together, or climbed into the car, each of us through his assigned door. It made him happy for all three of us to see the Sidoni bakery owner and his two sons in their own car, which was the same brand as ours but a different colour, and for each of us to speak with each of them, talking quickly because the cars were going in different directions. Ideally, he liked us to finish our conversation before the cars went their separate ways.

52

My brother's body still looked good at Ramez's wedding. The guests danced in the cramped and crowded space, circling around him and leaning in for a dance. He blocked them off, and hiding his face behind his raised forearms, looked even better, because his loose white shirt appeared as though it was tailor-made for that specific movement.

He never spoke a word to the girls who danced around him, or those who tried to dance with him, but just smiled at them or tossed his head back and laughed. Muhammad stood next to him and clapped off beat, then whispered in my brother's ear that he should talk to them or dance with one of them, or at least let some of them dance with him. But my brother didn't answer, just smiled and clapped.

Soon, the girls went off and danced far away from my brother, and Muhammad went to Ramez, who was sitting in a high armchair, and told him that my brother didn't know how to talk to women. Muhammad swept his body with his hands, saying that my brother was just for show. Ramez laughed hard at this, and I could see his smile from far away since his teeth seemed to get bigger and longer from smoking, which had also weakened his gums and lengthened his face.

Ramez gave Muhammad a look whenever he saw a girl sit down

from exhaustion, motioning for him to go and talk to her before she felt energetic and started dancing again. From his post on the high armchair, Ramez threw me a rose he'd picked up from the basket in front of him. It fell between the guests before it reached me, and he winked, telling me about the time I went to the airport with him, the day he travelled to Egypt. He made an airplane with his hand and pretended it was taking off, reminding me of all the fun we used to have. He was going to say something else, but one of his brothers whispered something in his ear, and he whispered something back. All of a sudden it became clear to me that because of this wedding, he was finally considered an adult like his brothers.

He got up and went into the dining hall, organising the food and the tables, and when he stayed for too long the guests chanted for him to come back. They sang and clapped for him, ignoring the song that was already playing. He hurried back and sat in his seat, and they chanted again and asked him to come down and dance with them and with his new bride. Soon, he got them all to relax and go back to their dancing, by waving his arms, lifting them up to his ears like a singer, and hugging his armchair and pretending he was afraid of them all and wanted to go back to the dining hall.

53

Because of the new oven, the window my father had put in the wall to make it easier to communicate with the table workers was now a window for transporting links of bread to the counter. Radwan stood by the window, but my father said he was the only one allowed to open and close it. Sometimes he threateningly told Radwan to keep his eyes on his work and not be distracted by the window opening and shutting. Other times, my father would slam the window shut in lieu of slamming his fist against Radwan's face, which stared and gawked at female customers. My father told Radwan he'd fire him and replace him with the dough-worker who swept and cleaned, obediently doing any extra work my father asked of him. Nawwaf stood in the front of the bakery, but in a different position from his old one. He worked on his old machine, which the inventor hadn't bothered to add to the new oven, and had to walk to the front of the counter for my father to see him. Nawwaf stood grasping the machine's handle and turning it. My father watched him stare into the machine, waiting to see how much water to add to the flour in it. He had to call him twice by his name. 'Nawwaf, Nawwaf,' he said, and Nawwaf looked up over his machine. My father made a big fist with one hand and a small fist with the other to let Nawwaf know his dough balls were too big. Then my father ran out to the counter, escaping the new oven's loud noises. He stood in the doorway and bent his ears to the street's sounds, and the breeze that carried them. Sometimes he stepped down and stood on the sidewalk, facing the bakery's storefront. Whenever a customer came to the door, my father hurried to open it for him. If anyone inside the bakery saw them both come in, they thought they were both customers, or that they'd walked down to the bakery together.

My uncle didn't like that. He only went to the counter to pick up loaves of bread for delivery. When my aunt's husband came, my father asked him how he was supposed to just stand at the counter and wait if there weren't any customers.

He sat in a chair by the drawer and the flour bags, and kept himself busy taking out loaves of bread from the small window and stacking them on the shelves, getting them ready for my uncle's deliveries, and enjoying the fact that now my uncle would see that he'd been working in his absence. The delivery truck took the bread to the grocery stores, and *they* sold the bread to customers. As for the small desserts, we started buying them from patisseries since our new oven didn't fit their huge metal trays and they couldn't handle the heat of the new oven anyway. A female customer asked my father if the desserts were fresh before she brought her mouth close to taste them. My father didn't know what to say, and the customer didn't know what she had just tasted. She told my father the dessert was stale, and held it in her hand not knowing whether to toss it aside, give it back to my father, or put it on the corner of the marble countertop for my father to deal with later.

Abu Qassem came in and comforted my father with stories about the bakeries of Ras Beirut. He told him that the Hamra bakery had was about to close, and that the owners of the Comodor bakery fought and split up. My father made to get up from his chair, and Abu Qassem told him to sit back down, but my father rose and went to the back room. He watched Nawwaf, the bakery's last and only employee, running back and forth and raising his shoulders to hide his bare neck from my father's palms. My father motioned for him to come – motioning had become his only way of communication –

and Nawwaf wiped his hands clean of the dough that clung to them. Then he looked down at his clothes to make sure that they were clean and free of any trace of flour.